ii

Marrin's Masquerade
By,
Julie Morrill

ISBN:978-1-968792-59-6

Acknowledgments

I am deeply grateful to my Aunts Laurie and Judy, whose encouragement and belief in my writing have been a blessing to me.

Special thanks to my long-time friend, mentor, and editor, Lynn Leissler. Your guidance, wisdom, and unwavering support have helped bring my stories to life. Let's keep on writing!

To my sister, Janie Richmond, whose own literary talents have inspired me more than I can say.

Finally, to all the friends and readers who have cheered me on along the way. Thank you for your love and support.

Dedication

For my husband, Pete — my muse, my greatest cheerleader, and the inspiration behind my romantic heroes. Thank you for your patience when I sometimes choose my keyboard over spending time with you.

I also dedicate this book to God, whose guidance, love, and grace inspire the stories I love to share.

CHAPTER 1:
Crossing the Atlantic

"He had discovered a great law of human action… that in order to make a man covet a thing, it is only necessary to make the thing difficult to attain." Mark Twain, *Tom Sawyer*

Somewhere in the Atlantic Ocean, Spring 1894

Marrin had spent the morning wandering the dim corridors of steerage, pretending to search for fresh air while quietly seeking any unguarded exit. Most doors were bolted or watched, but near the laundry room, she found a narrow crew passageway that smelled of coal dust and seawater. Heart pounding, she slipped into the shadowed alcove and discovered a steep iron maintenance ladder leading upward. With all the stealth she could muster—a challenging feat for someone with the grace and poise of a gangly, uncoordinated ostrich—she kicked aside her drab, cumbersome petticoat and began to climb, inching one foot above the other on the cold, greasy rungs. Nearing the top, she risked a peek over the smooth wooden deck as a soft, salt-mist breeze caressed her face.

A gull cried overhead, and footsteps clacked nearby. She ducked, holding her breath, waiting before daring to poke her head up again. But then… Her fingers slipped on the top rung. Hanging and swinging by one arm for a heartbeat, she managed to grab hold again and steady herself, panting as she closed her eyes and hugged the bars, waiting for her breath to calm. Slowly, shakily, she glanced at the dark, empty space below—and instantly regretted it. She swallowed hard and forced herself to look back up. Looking down was a very bad idea. She hefted her skirt over one shoulder and pulled herself up onto the wooden surface with an inelegant grunt. She landed in an awkward sprawl.

Wobbling to her feet, Marrin found herself tucked into a small corner of the promenade deck, safely hidden behind a low wall. She exhaled in relief, shook out her short, faded skirt, and lifted her chin, willing herself to look like she belonged as she stepped into view.

A steward appeared with an armful of towels, his narrowed gaze catching on her. Before he could speak, she ducked back behind the wall and down the ladder, peeking out just long enough to see him glance around, shake his head, and move on.

She carefully, cautiously climbed out again, looked in all directions for any sign of stewards or other ship crew, and stepped boldly, yet shakily across the deck to the rail, where she stood straight and tall, stiff but resolute, drinking in the briny air and blinking at the sunlight dancing across endless rolling waves of silver.

Marrin tucked chaotic, wind-tossed curls behind her ears; then she tightened her fingers on the railing as the ship listed to one side. She raised her face to clouds that billowed and swept across a milk-blue sky, teased and pushed by impish zephyrs. Closing her eyes, she felt the peek-a-boo sunlight that warmed her skin. Alone and utterly on her own for the long crossing of the Atlantic, she drank in the brief refreshment of the moment. Steerage passengers weren't allowed on this deck, but she desperately needed the air to think. And maybe to pray to a God she didn't really trust.

As her eyelids flicked open, the sea lay like an eternity around her. But she didn't have the luxury or safety of forever. America loomed in her future like a gathering hurricane.

"You'll work for four years in Virginia. Your indenture will help cover our debts, save our house, and save your sister." Her uncle's words clawed at her brain like a caged wild animal. "You will be *obedient* to your new masters. You owe it to us."

He'd shoved the ticket into her hand on the platform at Le Havre, his fingers taut, his tone merciless, unfeeling. No goodbye.

Her jaw clenched at the memory of him yanking her chin, of the way he spat *obedient*.

She had been obedient. She had boarded the ship, but she had no intention of selling herself into slavery in some far-off land. She would escape her indenture and find work so she could return to save her sister from their cruel aunt and uncle.

Poor little Robinette. Her younger sister's round cheeks, wide and worried, had stared out from a window of their aunt and uncle's mansion as Marrin was stuffed into a carriage before being whisked to the port.

Would they sell her sister, too?

Their parents had died when Marrin was twelve and Robinette only seven, leaving the sisters at the mercy of their aunt and uncle, *well,* leaving *her* at their mercy, anyway. They had loved Robinette, coddled her, treated her like a daughter, while Marrin had been little more than a servant.

Her thumb rubbed absently over the callouses in her palm. A lump rose in her throat, but she forced it down. There was no time for self-pity. What really frightened her was the thought of Robinette changing—becoming a pampered, spoiled girl who might one day look down on her—and others.

Her uncle had said someone would be waiting at Customs in New York Harbor with Marrin's name on a sign.

They would have to wait. She wouldn't be there.

She had no money and no fine clothes. However, she did have two things of value. She had taught herself to read, albeit in French, and she could act. Years of playing the submissive servant had been the perfect rehearsal. She'd studied the wealthy coming and going from her aunt and uncle's house—the haughty tip of their heads, the calm command in their voices, the way they carried themselves. Now she'd take on a new role. If she looked like she belonged in this part of the ship, like a first-class passenger, maybe—just maybe—she could blend with the nobler set, walk off this ship, vanish into the city, and find work and shelter in New York.

Eventually, she'd find her way back to Amiens, France. Back to Robinette—her only true family. She'd visit in secret, kidnap her, and do whatever she could to care for her.

The ship rocked again, pitching her sideways. She grabbed the rail and pulled herself upright. She was clumsy enough on dry land; on the rolling, dipping open sea, she was a disaster waiting to happen.

Turning her back to the sea, she leaned on the rail, eyes scanning the deck with casual ease, searching for an opportunity. Searching for a plan.

Over the next few days, she scrubbed her face and kept her hands meticulously clean. She straightened her posture, followed what little etiquette she knew, and twisted her thick, curly brunette hair into a neat bun—though it continually escaped by mid-morning, no matter how hard she tried to keep it under control.

Lovers strolled arm in arm. Mothers and daughters with parasols tread primly on promenades. Men strolled casually, smoking cigars and discussing business ventures. Neatly dressed children ran and played, closely guarded by governesses. The wealthy seemed to drift through life with a confidence and privilege she could only imagine.

Lucky for her, she had imagination to spare. And she had invested years picturing herself as one of them. Her parents hadn't been rich, but they hadn't been poor either. And her mother always had a sort of natural, wealthy air about her. Marrin, her beloved mother. Her namesake.

Lifting her chin, Marrin brushed a tear from her cheek, dropped her shoulders, and peered down her nose. She feigned boredom and cast a casual glance at a man and woman sitting on a nearby bench. The couple was clearly enthralled in a private, romantic tête-à-tête.

Eventually, the couple stood and walked away, disappearing behind an upended lifeboat. Left behind, draped over the bench, was the woman's lightweight linen summer coat of pale, creamy yellow—the loose-weave fabric flapping in the breeze.

Marrin's heart thumped faster. She strolled to the bench and seated herself primly in front of the coat, nonchalantly leaning her body against it. Shoulders back, head up, ugly boots tucked beneath the skirt that did little to conceal them.

Turning calmly, she deftly pulled the coat from behind her and spread it across her lap. She fingered the fine linen and lifted it to her cheek, inhaling its soft, lavender fragrance. Her hands traced the cool, smooth threads, the rows of fabric-covered buttons, the exquisite decorative cording on the sleeves. A label sewn inside read that it had been made in Paris.

The lovely pale color contrasted sharply with her navy wool skirt, yet it nicely complemented her pale blue blouse.

As another brisk breeze swept across the deck, she stood, adroitly donned the coat, and buttoned it so that it nearly covered her dark wool skirt. It was a perfect fit. Wrapped in that simple, delicate butteriness, she truly felt like a first-class passenger.

Except for her cloggy boots. If anyone asked, she'd say

they were her walking shoes—but she prayed no one would notice.

Lips twitching with a mixture of guilt and excitement, she ventured further along the deck, relaxing her countenance into one of genteel ennui. If the owner caught her wearing it, she'd wrinkle her nose with contempt and say she'd bought it in Paris over a year ago.

Two waiters stepped through a door onto the steamer's deck, carrying silver trays of hors d'oeuvres and glasses of water. They approached Marrin without the slightest hint of suspicion and asked if she'd care for a refreshment.

This was new.

Quelling her astonishment, she politely accepted a small paper napkin upon which lay a cracker topped with pâté and cheese. She took a glass of water and stood beside a tall, round café table to enjoy the refreshment.

When she finished her snack, she walked on, rounding another bend where she encountered the windward side of the ship. She was about to turn and escape the sharp blasts that whipped her hair wildly when she heard a girl shouting in French.

"I can't go. I simply cannot!"

Marrin stopped and watched a girl standing alone, speaking to no one but herself. Her arms were crossed defiantly, and her stylish navy-and-white-striped traveling dress flapped madly in the wind. In a dramatic flurry, the sophisticate ran to the side of the ship and folded herself over the deck's railing.

"I will not go!" she shouted again, gripping the rail with both hands and stepping onto the bottom rung, leaning precariously over the side.

Impulsively, Marrin ran to her. "Are you well, mademoiselle?" she asked gently, standing cautiously behind her.

The histrionic young lady fell back heavily against Marrin, nearly toppling them both. Marrin propped her up and half-dragged her to a nearby bench, where she patted the girl's cheeks and stroked her shoulders.

"I'll be all right," the girl replied, scowling as she pushed Marrin away and glared into her face for the first time.

An eerie shudder passed through Marrin, and she sucked in her breath, staring into the girl's eyes that blinked in a pallid face. Brown hair, fair skin, slim build. She saw herself. It was like looking into a mirror.

CHAPTER 2:
The Doppelgänger

"There comes a time in every rightly-constructed boy's life when he has a raging desire to go somewhere and dig for hidden treasure." Mark Twain, *Tom Sawyer*

This strange girl's eyes were blue instead of brown, and her hair was smooth and straight, whereas Marrin's was a mess of thick curls. Aside from these small details, however, the two young ladies were remarkably similar.

"Who are you?" the girl asked sharply.

"Marrin Fournier, mademoiselle," Marrin whispered shakily with a little bow of the head. "But I prefer to be called Marrin."

"Marrin." The corners of the girl's mouth tugged downward. "Why are you bowing your head to me like a common maid?"

"Sorry," she stammered. She had to stop doing and saying things that would give her away.

"You think I'm crazy, don't you?" the lookalike girl demanded, sitting up, apparently fully recovered from whatever had ailed her.

"No." Marrin twisted her long, thick hair into a ball behind her neck to keep it from blowing into her face. Did the girl not notice their resemblance? But Carina was studying her now—really studying her—eyes narrowing with a flicker of confusion, as if comparing Marrin's features to her own and not quite knowing what to make of it.

"Where are you from, Marrin?"

"Amiens, France."

"Where are you going?"

"America."

"I figured America. *Where* in America?"

"Virginia."

"How old are you? Eighteen?"

"Nearly," Marrin answered. "Who are you?" It was Marrin's turn to ask questions.

"Carina Lejeune of Antwerp," she replied with more than a hint of arrogance.

Marrin resisted the urge to bow her head again in deference to the girl's aristocratic manner.

"And where are you going, Mademoiselle Lejeune?"

"Your coat is positively scrumptious. But what kind of shoes are those?" Carina demanded, pointing to her feet and ignoring the inquiry.

Marrin flushed, turned her toes inward, and lifted her chin defiantly. "They're my traveling shoes. And you didn't answer my question."

"Nice *traveling* shoes," Carina snorted. "They look more like farm boots. And why are you out in the sun without a parasol?"

"It's too windy. And…And you're here without a parasol," Marrin retorted.

"That's because I was thinking of throwing myself overboard."

Marrin's breath caught. "Would you really have done it?"

Carina tossed her head and gave a short laugh. "No, of course not. I was only thinking of what Francine—my governess—would do if she found me on the railing… if the near-blind incompetent woman could even *see* me. I hoped she'd notice my desperation and take me back to Belgium."

Marrin studied her, uncertain whether Carina was joking or simply spoiled.

"You still haven't answered my question," Marrin said firmly.

"What question?" Carina circled her, conducting an examination from every angle.

"Where are you going?"

"Tell me your story first, and then I'll tell you where *I'm* going." Carina wrinkled her nose at Marrin's boots. "And I know you have a story."

Marrin hesitated, fingering the gold locket about her neck before plunging forward. She opened the tri-fold locket. "My parents are dead, and I'm being sent to Virginia to live with complete strangers." She pointed to the photographs and described her parents and sister, Robinette.

Carina grabbed and squeezed Marrin's hands. "Oh, my dear!" she exclaimed, her face too close as her eyes blinked what appeared to be sudden and genuine concern. "I'm sorry for your loss. And I can sympathize with being sent away to a foreign land to live with complete strangers."

"Thank you," Marrin muttered, startled at Carina's show of compassion. "They actually died years ago, but…"

"I might as well be an orphan," Carina interrupted. "I've been at boarding school most of my life and barely know my parents. Now they're sending me to some ridiculously tiny town in California to live with a farmer uncle who doesn't even know me. Sent off to live with strangers, just like you."

"Why would they send you away?" Marrin wanted to know. Her own aunt and uncle, back in France, made her wary of trusting anyone.

Carina pouted. "I got into the slightest bit of trouble at school, and they want me to 'learn a lesson' by living on a *farm* in the Wild West." She spat the word *farm* like it was bitter on her tongue. She folded her arms. "Can you imagine living on a farm like a peasant? I refuse to go. I've been formulating a plan. I have a fiancé back home in Brussels." She sighed, clasping her hands to her breast. "Well, *almost* fiancé. More of a serious suitor. His name is Anton. He's so handsome and wonderful. Anyhow, I'll pretend to lose my identification papers so Francine will have to take me back to Belgium, where I'll run away with Anton."

"How long are you supposed to stay with this uncle of yours in California?" Marrin asked, ignoring Carina's starry-eyed romanticism.

Carina pouted. "Knowing my parents, they'll forget about me and leave me there forever."

Marrin could understand that. Aside from facing indentured servitude, rather than living on a farm, she was in a similar situation. "Do you have other family?"

"Besides this uncle in California?" Carina asked. "Yes, a mean, selfish older brother I care nothing for. His name is Alard. He moved to America several years ago. He lives somewhere on the East Coast, last I heard." She huffed. "Your turn. Tell me about yourself."

Marrin took a breath. "My aunt and uncle are sending me away to be an indentured servant in Virginia," she said miserably.

"No!" Carina gasped.

Marrin nodded. "They sold me as a slave to pay off their debts. I have to work for an American family for four years."

"Quelle horreur!" Carina exclaimed, her eyes wide with sympathy. "I guess that explains your shoes." Marrin nodded. Carina put a consoling arm around her shoulders and squeezed.

"You cannot debase yourself and become…" Carina wrinkled her nose and flourished a hand toward the stairwell leading to the lower decks. "…one of the *steerage*. But you must admit, your story is tragically romantic." She gave Marrin another squeeze.

"Hm," said Marrin. She pulled herself from Carina's embrace and stuffed her hands into the pockets of the linen summer coat. Her fingers touched something curious.

Was she convincing Carina that she was from a wealthier class? "My story is tragic, yes," Marrin said. "Romantic, no." A gust of wind loosed a curly lock, tossing it into her eyes as she looked out to sea.

"Carina Maria Lejeune!" The name cracked like a whip from the lips of Carina's governess.

Carina kept her back turned to Francine and looked at Marrin, sticking out her tongue and crossing her eyes.

Marrin pursed her lips and suppressed a giggle.

"Don't you ever leave my side again, young lady," Francine scolded, glaring at… *Marrin*! Francine's pince-nez sat crookedly on her nose, and she squinted as though everything were a blur.

Marrin's breath caught, and she placed a questioning hand on her chest.

"Don't you play innocent with me, Miss Lejeune." Carina still had her back to the governess, brows furrowing as her brain registered Francine's error. "And what on earth are you wearing?" She squinted and bent at the waist. "Where did you get those ugly boots?"

The lookalike whispered in an exaggerated accent, "Now's our chance! Go with Francine. Try being me for a while—see what happens. She's so clueless, she won't notice the difference between you and me."

Then Carina darted away, slipping behind a group of promenading ladies just as Francine straightened.

"You must get rid of those boots immediately," Francine scolded. "They look as though they came from a rummage bin."

Marrin froze, stunned. Carina had acted with the reckless confidence of someone who had always gotten her way. And now Marrin was alone—with Carina's governess—expected to play a role she'd never rehearsed.

She didn't know what to do or how to behave.

"You are in a great deal of trouble, young lady," Francine said sharply, seizing her arm and pulling her through a door into the ship's interior.

Marrin's feet immediately turned to lead, and she was unable to take another step. They had entered a palatial lounge with a high ceiling and walls decorated with bronze sconces and grand mirrors. Ornate windows of colorful stained glass were interspersed with tall, wide bay windows that looked out onto the sea.

Francine put her lips to Marrin's ear. "Don't you dare make me look a fool in front of all these people, Carina. Move your cloddy peasant feet and come along this instant."

Marrin awakened from her stupor and managed to stumble behind Francine as they proceeded past groups of handsomely dressed men and women seated on plush green velvet sofas and armchairs. She stumbled inelegantly as the floor moved and pitched beneath her worn boots. Out of the corner of an eye, she glimpsed a disapproving, spectacled squint peering at her over the top of a newspaper. She stared down self-consciously; then raised her head again to take in the opulence of the room. She didn't want to miss this.

Her aunt and uncle's villa in Amiens was quite lovely, but never had she seen anything as lavish as this. It was as though she'd stepped into the Versailles Palace itself.

Francine jerked Marrin up a beautifully carpeted staircase and down a narrow corridor before stopping at a door. She released Marrin long enough to pull a key from her skirt pocket.

"We have an hour to get you bathed and dressed for luncheon," said Francine, opening the door and waving Marrin inside.

Carina's cabin. It was a small, yet beautiful suite with soft carpet and carved wood paneling painted white. Two narrow beds stood side by side. She assumed one was Carina's and the other was where Francine slept. A small, round table and two chairs sat in one corner, and a long, narrow steel tub stood in another beside a wash basin and a short stool stacked with plush towels.

"Comb out your disastrous hair while I go order hot water to be brought up for your bath," Francine called over her shoulder as she departed. "And don't you dare go anywhere."

Marrin wasn't about to leave. If pretending to be Carina for an hour or two meant a hot bath, clean clothes, and a delicious meal, she was more than ready for this game.

As she soaked blissfully in the warm water, staring up at a crystal ceiling sconce amidst a smattering of filigree whorls, her mind raced with impossible possibilities. The resemblance between her and Carina was uncanny. It made her wonder....

Wearing a dainty pair of white leather boots and a lovely afternoon gown—one of pale mint fabric with enormous gigot sleeves that looked like two hot air balloons about to carry her away, Marrin sat slurping from a bowl of potato soup as Carina's governess prattled on. Only occasionally did Francine stop to reprimand Marrin's poor manners or condemn her for gawking like this was her first time on a luxury steamer.

"And what has happened to that frightful hair of yours?" Francine asked between quiet, refined spoonfuls of soup. "This ocean air seems to have curled it into an obscenity."

A waiter replaced the soup bowls with plates of poached cod Hollandaise fringed with steamed potatoes and carrots. Marrin took the moment to glance about the dining room in search of Carina. Where had she gone? What was she eating for luncheon? Would she grow hungry and suddenly appear to ruin Marrin's revelry in first-class nobility?

But Carina never appeared, leaving Marrin to the joy of a wonderful night's sleep, aside from the governess's intermittent nocturnal snorts and lip smacks. They were far more bearable than the loud, obnoxious snores of bunked passengers and the intermittent crying of babies in the crowded dormitory below deck.

And as she lay on the gently rocking ship, she stared up at the moonlight glistening through the porthole onto the crystal sconce above the bed. What if she could trade lives with Carina? What if she could escape her indenture in Virginia and start anew with Carina's uncle on his farm in California? What if…?

CHAPTER 3:
The Switch

"Courage is resistance to fear, mastery of fear—not absence of fear." — Mark Twain's *Pudd'nhead Wilson's Calendar* (1894)

*M*arrin shaded her eyes with a hand, scanning the waves, peering up and down the promenade deck. Francine had returned to their state room to fetch parasols that would protect them from the bright morning rays.

"I can help you," said Carina in a breathy whisper, startling Marrin where she sat on a bench.

"We can help each other."

"Carina!" she gasped. "Where have you been?"

"Having the time of my life, thank you very much."

"Where did you sleep?"

"I asked one of the maids to please let me sleep in an empty room for the night. I told her who I was, what room I was in, and complained that I couldn't sleep because of my governess's snoring, et voilà! Of course, it helped that I slipped her a few coins. A room and bath all to myself for the night! I ordered meals brought up so I could enjoy them in private." She hugged herself. "Heaven."

"Ingenious," Marrin said, though unease twisted in her stomach.

"Speaking of genius…" Carina's eyes darted furtively. "We have to go." She tugged Marrin from the bench and dragged her clear around to the opposite side of the ship, where they flopped panting onto another bench.

"The old, befuddled bat won't find us here," said Carina. "As I was saying, you and I look alike, and my Uncle Liam Stinson has never seen me."

"I could take your place and go to live with him in California, so you can return home to be with Anton?" asked Marrin, her voice excited.

"Our minds think alike!" Carina exclaimed. "We can trade identification papers," she continued. "There has to be a way we can make this work."

Hope surged in Marrin's chest, only to collide with a wall of dread. "But first, tell me about this uncle of yours. What is he like?"

Carina placed a comforting hand on her wrist. "I've never met him. All I know is that he was born in Belgium and moved to America many years ago. Mother says he's well-off and lives alone since his wife died. He'll probably be glad to have company."

Marrin sucked in her lower lip as a breeze caught her hair and splashed a waterfall of curls into her face. "I'd certainly have a better life with him than as a slave." She exhaled slowly. "What do you think? Can we do this?"

"I think we can," Carina nodded eagerly.

Marrin had already made up her mind that pretending to be Carina was a far better plan than indentured servitude, but what if Carina changed her mind or was forcibly sent back to California? What if Carina's parents showed up there and exposed Marrin as a fraud? At best, she'd go to jail. At worst, she'd be sent to her slaveholders in Virginia.

"What about your governess?" asked Marrin. "Will she ever figure out that I'm not you?"

"Not likely," she sniffed. "She hasn't noticed yet, has she?"

Marrin shook her head. "How will I get to California?"

"Francine will take you to the train station, buy you a ticket, and put you on the train headed west. As soon as I debark, I'll buy another ticket on board a steamer returning to Europe."

"But not the same ship your governess will be on," said Marrin.

"No, Francine is taking a train to Montreal, Canada to visit a friend or relative. She's not sailing back to Belgium for another week."

"Do you have money for passage back to Europe?"

Carina opened the velvet drawstring purse in her lap to reveal a roll of American dollar bills. She flipped through it and handed a portion to Marrin. "Here. You may need this. And, yes, I have plenty of money to get back home."

Marrin took the bills, staring at them before shoving them into a pocket of her dress. *Carina's* dress. "You're sure you can manage customs and all your luggage on your own?" Marrin asked.

"Right," said Carina, scrunching her lips. "You could take all my luggage except my nicest dresses, of course. I'll take those back with me. Anton will buy me plenty more things, I'm sure."

"What if your governess discovers that your identification papers aren't yours before we leave the ship?" Marrin's pulse quickened. "There might be a search for all passengers' papers before we're allowed to debark."

Carina waved a hand as if brushing away a gnat. "The old crone once mistook a complete stranger for me at the opera and didn't notice for half an hour. This will work, I promise."

But Marrin had more questions. "What about your brother, Alard? What if he tries to find you in California and finds me instead?"

"He wouldn't recognize you—or me, rather. He hasn't seen me since I was small. Besides, he would never come looking for me. He's a selfish beast and cares for no one but himself. He left several years ago and never wrote to us. We heard rumors he was leading a life of crime. An outlaw, or some such thing."

A shiver tingled down Marrin's spine. An outlaw? She didn't want to imagine what such a man might do.

"I need to learn how to be you," said Marrin.

Carina grabbed Marrin by both shoulders and grinned. "From now on, you are officially Carina Maria Lejeune of Antwerp." She clapped her hands together and took a deep breath. "Now, let me teach you all about myself."

That won't be difficult for you, Marrin thought.

"My mother—I mean now *your* mother," Carina giggled, "was born Giselle Laverne Stinson of Bernissart, Belgium."

"Your Uncle Liam's sister," Marrin commented.

"That's right." Carina pouted. "I'm sure Uncle Liam is nicer than my mother. She's all impatience and self-importance. Uncle Stinson speaks fluent French and English, so that's helpful for you. Oh, and he's Protestant."

"I'm Protestant," said Marrin.

"But my family is Catholic. Maybe you can say you converted to Protestantism when you made a friend at boarding school. My parents would pitch a fit, but—"

"Boarding school?"

"Oh, yes. Sint-Katelijne-Waver in Antwerp. Catholic, of course. I'll tell you about it."

She rambled on. About school, friends, parents, her brother, clothes—and, of course, far too much about her beloved fiancé, Anton. *How will I remember all this?* Marrin worried. *What if I forget important details? What if Carina's uncle in California tests me and I fail somehow?*

"You must occasionally make the sign of the cross before meals like I do," said Carina, showing her the ritual gesture.

"I'll tell your Uncle Stinson that I'm Protestant."

"It'll be more convincing that you're me if you make the sign of the cross occasionally," Carina argued. "Just say it's a hard habit to break."

Marrin practiced. She did it backward—right shoulder first instead of left.

"You're clearly not Catholic," Carina chuckled.

Marrin's throat thickened. She couldn't get this wrong! She'd never try it anyhow.

As the lunch hour approached, Carina disguised Marrin by wrapping a shawl around her head and making her walk hunched over like an old lady. Carina pretended to assist her. The last thing they wanted was to draw the attention of gawkers, making a fuss about lookalikes. And, if Carina's governess saw them together, everything would be spoiled.

"We should get you a cane," said Carina, laughing. She invited Marrin to a table in a small, yet opulent parlor in first class, where they could sit unobserved and enjoy a light fare of tuna sandwiches, crisped rye crackers, and crudité. It was also a place where Carina could continue to talk about herself, while Marrin took copious notes with a pencil and a small notepad given to her by a steward. Though she didn't have much of an education, she was proud of her brief time in school while her parents were alive. At least she could read and write, if only at a low level.

When Carina paused for a breath, Marrin felt the loquacious girl's eyes burning into her.

"What?" Marrin asked.

"How long did you say you've been orphaned?"

"My parents died several years ago."

Carina's lips curled into a scowl. "I guess that explains your poor table etiquette."

Marrin looked up in alarm. "What do you mean?" she asked, swiping at a bit of food on her chin.

"Ugh," Carina groaned, "if you're going to pretend to be me, you can't eat like a stable peasant." She gestured disdainfully at Marrin's fork. "Hold it properly. And, for heaven's sake, sit up straight."

Marrin's cheeks burned. Carina was scolding her as much as Francine had. She gripped her fork more tightly, as if manners could be absorbed through her fingers.

"It's obvious you never attended boarding school." Carina paused before whining about how much she missed Anton. Marrin heard nothing as she worried that her lack of etiquette would reveal her as a charlatan.

"There's the matter of our agreement," Marrin interrupted when she could get a word in edgewise. She wanted something in writing. Proof of their arrangement, in case Carina's uncle got suspicious. "We need to write out our plan and sign it to prove we mutually agreed to this conspiracy."

Carina agreed to the proposition, and Marrin hauled in a gallon of air as *her hand drifted to the gold locket at her neck. Would this work? Would Carina back out of the plan and ruin her chance at freedom?*

A sour, oily stench clung to the low ceilings as Marrin descended into steerage. The air pressed on her chest—thick with sweat, smoke, and something vaguely rotten. Leaving the polished world above felt like shedding a costume, yet slipping back into the familiar crush of languages and weary faces gave her a strange sense of relief.

Here, at least, she could let down her guard and stop pretending to be someone she wasn't. The loud laughter, the drab-rag clothing, the swirl of French, English, Italian, Polish, and German—this cacophony of survival felt familiar. But how could she sustain a double life for weeks, even months? Lies were not part of her nature, yet somehow, they had already woven themselves into her days.

There was also some reprieve in once again letting down her guard and laying aside her pretense of being someone she was not. Back amongst a mixture of different languages, they were at least a familiar class of people, with their loud laughter and drab rag clothing. Voices rose in French, English, Italian, Polish, and German—overlapping in a loud, familiar cacophony of survival. How would she ever lead a double life for weeks and months at a time? Lies were not part of her nature, yet they'd begun to be part of her everyday life.

Still adorned in Carina's day dress, Marrin stood out like a rose amongst thorns. Other passengers gaped, deferring to her as though she were royalty—and probably wondering what a first-class passenger was doing in steerage.

"Who are you, and what are you doing visiting us down here?" asked her bunkmate in an attempt at French.

"I belong down here," she replied. "I just happen to have a nice dress." The girl shrugged, sighed, and rolled over on the bunk. Marrin's heart began to calm again. She was thankful no one was asking too many questions. Still, she feared that her bunkmate might try to steal her clothes if she removed them, so she slept in them all night. She lay awake for a long time, wondering how her scheme would play out.

The following morning, Marrin escaped to the upper deck and made her way to Carina's cabin, where the two young ladies drafted two copies of their plan and signed their names to the documents—after they spent some time practicing each other's signatures. Then Marrin tried on a lovely new dress and stylish boots that fit her perfectly. She stood before a mirror and patted her hair, coiffed in the latest fashionable Gibson style, thanks to Carina's handiwork. But when Carina's reflection appeared beside hers, she jumped.

"I know," said Carina. "The resemblance is uncanny."

Marrin nodded, *thinking she barely recognized herself in the mirror.*

"This is my chance to be back home with the man I love," said Carina, breaking Marrin's reverie.

And what was her own chance? Marrin didn't know yet, but it was more than she'd ever dared to hope for.

At that moment, the impoverished, orphaned Marrin Fournier disappeared, and she became Miss Carina Lejeune of Antwerp, Belgium—destined for California, freedom, and a future yet unwritten.

CHAPTER 4:
The Masquerade Begins

"The world seemed a wilderness full of lurking dangers."
Mark Twain's *Tom Sawyer*

*M*arrin sucked in a juddered breath, stuck out her chin, and squared her shoulders. Adorned in one of Carina's finely tailored traveling dresses, she truly looked and felt the part of a first-class passenger. Mentally, she prepared herself to make her way through Customs with Carina's governess. Then she'd travel to the train station and begin her adventure across America to California. An excited smile fought to break out on her lips. If only she had a map of the United States to gain some perspective on just how far she'd be traveling. A train ride across the entire country! What amazing adventures she was having!

As she and Francine joined the crowd of other passengers flooding the deck to peer out at New York Harbor, an exultant cheer arose at the sight of the famed Statue of Liberty, the great lady who welcomed everyone to America.

The collective sense of hope sent chills through her body. America. Would it offer a promising new start for her, too?

She spotted an oversized gauzy pink rosette hat

bobbing several yards away. Was it her doppelgänger? She couldn't be sure. They were both risking a lot. If their scheme failed, Marrin would be forced into slavery and might never see her sister again, while Carina might lose the love of her life forever. Their plan had to work.

Her hands tightened around the ship's railing, and her eyes stretched, overwhelmed by the vastness of New York City, the sparkling beauty of the harbor, the giant symbol of the friendship between the United States and France, the home she'd left behind.

The passengers crowding the deck waved hats and scarves, cheering, hugging one another, crying, "America! America!" Someone kissed her cheek in the jubilant chaos. Caught up in a surge of happiness, her heart almost forgot its trepidation.

Because she was no longer considered a steerage passenger, Marrin had no trouble obtaining health clearances and advancing through Customs, but as she did so, she looked back and saw that lower-class passengers were being held back, examined, and questioned more thoroughly. Several travelers were being forced into a quarantine area, where they might be deported back to their countries of origin. Carina would want to be deported. Maybe she'd pretend to be sick. Then she spied the girl. She'd been correct in guessing that Carina was wearing the rosette hat, but she was being detained by Customs officials. Marrin's knuckles suddenly turned white as she clutched her valise. What if Carina were forced to tell the truth of their exchanged identification papers? What if her Virginian master recognized Carina as Marrin and tried to force her into indenture?

Carina will be fine, she told herself as she pushed blindly through the throng. If Carina were caught, she could probably talk her way out of anything and reconnect with her governess or family. She'd be protected and safe. Marrin, however, would not. She had to protect herself.

The mass of people grew tighter as they slowly funneled through the doors of the building. Little by little, shuffle by shuffle, Marrin surged with hundreds of others onto a bridge connecting Ellis Island to the mainland. She emerged into the open air amidst a pressing chaos of foreign languages, whoops and shouts, the cries of seagulls, and the stink of body odor.

Standing on tiptoe, she peered over the crowd, searching for Carina. Where had she gone? What would become of her?

Then—there she was. Carina, unmistakable in her pink rosette hat, was being escorted back toward the ship by a steward. She turned, spotted Marrin through the swarm of passengers, and flashed an exuberant grin, waving with all the enthusiasm of someone being handed exactly what she wanted. She was going home. Back to Belgium. Back to the life she had almost lost.

Marrin released a breath she hadn't realized she was holding. She longed to wave back but didn't dare. If Francine turned and saw Carina, everything would collapse. From this moment forward, Marrin had to live—utterly and convincingly—as Carina Lejeune.

Looking ahead again, she followed Francine as closely as possible. In the sea of people on the dock was a man holding a sign bearing her name. Her *real* name. Her throat closed, and panic stole her breath. Though she told herself not to make eye contact, she couldn't help herself. She looked straight at the man, and his brows lifted. "Marrin Fournier?" he mouthed. She tightened her grip on her valise, flipped her chin forward, and marched past, pushing her pace. She was not Marrin Fournier, the indentured servant; she was the wealthy and privileged Carina Lejeune of Antwerp, Belgium.

Her mind shouted in warning not to look back at the Virginian man until her feet set foot on dry land.

"Carina!" Francine shouted, jogging to catch up to her.

She paused to cast a quick look backward, and her heart froze cold as she again locked eyes with her would-be captor. But there was no need to fear. Francine shouted Carina's name again and grabbed her by the elbow, scolding her to stay close. The Virginian stopped looking in her direction. Gulping deep breaths of air, she forced her shoulders to relax and steadied her breathing.

Next, onward to the luggage claim area on the pier, where they gathered their tagged belongings and stacked them into a pile. Francine hailed one of the many porters eager to make money assisting passengers. A very young boy of about twelve pushed an empty hand cart up to their luggage and began piling it onto the vehicle.

"Do you know where I…find train schedule?" Francine asked the boy in broken English.

The boy grinned, flashing rows of small white pearls as he yanked a pamphlet from his trouser pocket and handed it to her.

Francine pulled out her pocket watch. "We are here quite early this morning," she said to Marrin. "If we go directly to the station, you'll be there in plenty of time to take the afternoon train if there's room for you."

Marrin assented to the idea. Why wait around with Francine, who might become suspicious?

"Manhattan Train Station, please," The governess instructed the porter.

"Yes, ma'am," he said. "I'll take you to a taxi."

The boy was very adept at securing their luggage into the taxicab before reaching out his hand to assist Marrin and Francine into the conveyance. Francine paid the boy, and the cab lurched forward.

Marrin waved to the young porter, and he winked back, blowing a kiss. "Cheeky boy," she said, smiling. She smoothed the fabric of Carina's blue- and white-striped traveling dress and tucked a wayward curl behind an ear.

Enjoying the relief of safety and near-freedom at last,

she swept her eyes behind the jostling cab and spied the Virginian with the *Marrin Fournier* sign. Was he following her? She wrenched her head around and choked down a lump of fear, telling herself to focus. If the man confronted her, she'd simply show him her identification papers. She'd be fine.

The train station was thick with people, engine steam, and the echoing, chaotic din of hundreds of people coming and going. Francine bought her ticket and handed it to Marrin.

The words, *Transcontinental Railway* were splashed across the ticket. Marrin tucked it into her skirt pocket.

"Don't lose it," Francine commanded, frowning.

Marrin bit her cheek and ran her eyes over the crowd. She wanted to get this over with and board the train before the Virginian showed up—if he was indeed still in pursuit.

She took a deep breath. "Well, I suppose this is where we part."

Francine gave her an awkward hug. "In spite of all the years of trouble you've given me, Carina, I suppose I'm going to miss you a little."

"Oh," Marrin faltered. "I suppose I'll miss you too."

A whistle and the shout of "All aboard!" blasted beside them, making Marrin jump.

"Marrin Fournier?" a man's voice called out.

Her blood froze. She turned just enough to see him— the Virginian—pushing through the crowd, the sign with her name still in his hand.

Francine's mouth tightened. "Carina? What is going on?"

Before Marrin could speak, a police officer approached with the Virginian at his side.

"Marrin Fournier?" the officer asked.

Marrin lifted her chin, though her knees trembled. "Non."

"Identification papers, please."

Francine bristled. "This is absurd!"

Marrin fumbled for the papers in her skirt pocket. Her fingers shook as she handed them over. The officer inspected them, then held them up to the light, speaking in low tones with the Virginian.

The Virginian scowled, spat on the ground, and finally growled, "Not her." He turned and stalked away.

Only when he vanished into the crowd did the officer return the documents. "Apologies, miss," he said briskly, then moved on to the next passenger.

Marrin clutched the papers to her chest, dizzy with relief.

"That was completely ridiculous," Francine huffed. "Mistaken identity, clearly."

Marrin could only nod.

Not long after the incident, a train chugged into the station, piercing the air with its whistle and filling the building with clouds of steam. When the train drew to a hissing halt, a small team of stevedores scrambled to unload luggage and then reload the cavernous bellies of the train cars. At long last, a conductor blew his whistle and shouted, "All aboard!" Words Marrin had longed to hear.

Passengers formed queues and began boarding. Marrin glanced back at Francine before shuffling along the queue and disappearing into the train, where she held her breath and stepped into her luxurious private cabin. She slid open a window and waved a lace handkerchief to Carina's governess as her eyes searched for the Virginian. But he was nowhere to be seen.

The train whistled again, and the iron horse shuddered, jerked forward, and rocked her off balance. She was headed west. New name, new identity, new life.

Was this real? Was this actually happening? She had successfully escaped indentured servitude. She was free! But would she forget the girl she used to be? Marrin Fournier of Amiens, France? Yet perhaps now she could finally be her true self for the first time in a long, long time.

Cities, towns, and empty landscapes flew past the car window as Marrin voyaged across the United States. Homesickness had suddenly hit her hard. Her beloved Amiens, France, with its beautiful Somme River, colorful houses, and crisscrossing canals. Amiens, the home of the famous author Jules Verne, who wrote *Journey to the Center of the Earth, Twenty Thousand Leagues Under the Sea,* and *Around the World in Eighty Days.* She'd never read the books, but she'd always dreamed of doing so.

And she missed Robinette terribly—her bright, hopeful little sister who was only twelve and far too young to face the wickedness of the world alone. Would the Virginians wire her aunt and uncle when she didn't appear in New York? Of course they would. And what then? What if her aunt and uncle decided to sell Robinette into indentured servitude in her place? The thought made Marrin sick to her stomach. Robinette was only twelve. She'd never survive such a fate. If only she could find a way to write to her without the letter passing through her aunt and uncle's hands—and revealing her hiding place.

As the days passed, Marrin found herself completely spoiled in her Pullman car, where she was treated like royalty. The train was beyond even her wildest imagination—paneled in polished walnut, trimmed in brass so shiny she could see her reflection in it, and seats upholstered in deep emerald velvet. Other passengers enjoyed plush seating that folded into curtained sleeping berths at night, while Marrin indulged in her own private first-class compartment. Her conscience wrestled in a mix of delight and guilt. The former servant was now the one being served. She could get used to this.

At first, the porters startled her. She had never met

anyone with such deep, warm skin tones before; their bright eyes and gleaming smiles fascinated her. Meeting these elegant domestics of African descent made her feel both shy and deeply curious. The porter assigned to her car moved with poise and pride, yet there was a heaviness in his eyes— as though he carried the weariness of a thousand journeys. If only she could speak to him. She had so many questions she wanted to ask about his family, where he was from, and what place he called home.

As the train chugged westward, conversation filled the cars—a tumult of accents and stories, most of which she could not understand. A silver-haired couple from Boston marveled at the vastness of the woods and farmland. Two Englishmen argued daily about gold mining and money, their vowels round and polished. A fast-talking family from Massachusetts entertained their children with tales of buffalo hunts, prairie fires, and "wild Indians." Marrin listened quietly, soaking in the symphony of voices, flipping through her French-English dictionary, taking copious notes, and struggling to learn the language of this vast new country.

Each night, the porters transformed the little sitting rooms into cozy sleeping berths. In her narrow bed with its crisp sheets and soft, plump pillow, the rhythmic clatter of the rails lulled her to sleep.

Despite these comforts, Marrin's dreams were far from peaceful. She often awoke in panic, fretting over worst-case scenarios. What if Carina had been caught before she had a chance to return to Belgium to marry her fiancé? Would she be sent to California to her Uncle Stinson, and if so, what would he think if he saw both girls side by side? Would Marrin be sent to indentured servitude in Virginia? Or would she be deported back to France? Worse still, would she be put in jail? Yet none of that could happen if she explained to Carina's uncle how the two girls had willingly and mutually agreed to their charade. There was no real harm in what they were doing. Was there?

Each morning, Marrin's anticipation rose with the sunlight that gilded the patchwork of farms and forest beyond her window. She watched the world rushing by and felt her old life fading into the past, swallowed by the miles. Ahead lay California. Freedom. And the dangerous thrill of hope.

CHAPTER 5:
New Acquaintances

"It is curious that physical courage should be so common in the world and moral courage so rare." — Mark Twain, *Following the Equator* (1897)

A mid-afternoon breeze blew in a gust of warmth as Marrin disembarked from the train and stepped stiff-legged onto a platform at the depot on the outskirts of Yreka, California. Stretching and wiping sweaty palms on her skirt, she popped open her white lace parasol and cast a wide eye at disheveled cowboys and calico-clad women in sunbonnets and more plain and practical parasols who stared back at her with curiosity and a tinge of judgment on their faces. Once again, Marrin felt out of place. She smoothed her skirt and knew she was overdressed. How would she fit into this new place? She closed her fancy parasol and tucked it into a carpetbag. None of the other women was using parasols. She wore a wide-brimmed pancake hat, but she needed a sunbonnet.

Looking west toward town, Marrin was unimpressed. It was very small, looked newish, yet hastily built, and only a few buildings were painted at all.

Marrin ignored a man's voice shouting somewhere behind her. She stood on tiptoe to see further up Miner

Street and into the center of town. She wrung her hands to keep them from shaking. How could she do this? How could she play the part of a near stranger and expect to get away with it? "Carina Lejeune?" the man's voice called again. Oh, yes, that was her! She'd have to get used to her new name.

She spun round, her stare connecting with the pale, watery blue eyes of a man in his late thirties wearing a pair of worn dungarees. "Oui, monsieur," she said, bobbing a short curtsy. "I mean yes sir. I speak English."

The man slid a straw hat from his head and nodded to her with a demeanor so humble and kind that it was almost shy. Her gut swirled. Was this Mr. Liam Stinson? How could she lie to such a person? Then again, looks could be deceiving. He might be no different from her mean old uncle back home.

"Bienvenue en Californie, Mademoiselle Lejeune," he said, smiling and jutting his hand. She shook it uncertainly. He continued in French, "I'm your Uncle Liam Stinson. It's a pleasure to meet you. I'll speak to you in French as much as you need." He inclined his head. "Is this your luggage?"

"Oui, monsieur," she said, bobbing a short curtsy. She groped for the English words. "I mean—yes…sir. I…learn speak English."

"You *are* learning," he said warmly.

She ducked her head. "Only…tiny words."

Liam's smile was comforting. "We'll get you there." He instructed a rail station porter to load the trunk and satchels into the back of a smart two-seated surrey covered with a canvas canopy. "I hope you'll be happy here, Mademoiselle Lejeune," he said with warmth in his words.

"I'm sure I will be," she replied. She pressed her lips into a tense seam.

Mr. Stinson held out his hand for Marrin to sit in the front seat of the surrey before walking around to sit beside her. It was a little uncomfortable to be so close to a complete stranger, but he smelled faintly of soap and lavender, which was not unpleasant.

As the vehicle moved up a dusty road northward out of town, Marrin swiped a finger across her perspiring forehead and tried to steady her legs. Even in the warm, late spring weather, her limbs were shaking. She wasn't sure what to say or what might be polite or impolite, so she remained silent.

Thankfully, Mr. Stinson spoke first. "As you know, I lost my wife a few years back."

"Yes, I am sorry for you," said Marrin, attempting English.

"You're learning some English already!" he exclaimed with approval in his tone. "And thank you for your sympathy. Your Aunt Penelope," he continued with a crooked smile on his lips. "She was born in America. Always a jolly soul."

She blinked. "Jolly?" She asked, timidly rolling the word on her tongue. "Like… jolie? Pretty?"

He laughed. "Well, Penelope was certainly pretty," he said, "but jolly means happy. Heureuse. I'll go back to speaking French for now."

"Merci," she said.

"Your Aunt Penelope was a friend to all," he continued in Marrin's native tongue. "I miss her." He paused, swallowed, and spoke to his team, urging them a little faster. "Besides my cook and housekeeper, Edith, who comes out to work during the day, you'll be the only female living at Greenwind Ranch."

Marrin cleared her throat and shifted in her seat.

"Don't worry, Mademoiselle. All my men have been ordered to behave themselves and treat you with the utmost respect."

"Merci," she said again, gripping the side of her seat more firmly.

They rounded a hill and entered a wide, open span of

green prairie grass dotted with sparse juniper and oak trees. Marrin sucked in her breath sharply at the sight of a stunning snow-capped mountain towering in the distance. She'd seen the mountain from her train window, but seeing it like this was even more breathtaking, standing alone and proud like a silent giant.

"That's Mt. Shasta," Mr. Stinson explained with a sweep of his hand, "and this here is Shasta Valley."

"C'est magnifique," she breathed—then caught herself. "I mean…jolly."

Liam chuckled.

The openness of the landscape and the majesty of the mountain struck Marrin's heart with a sudden loneliness—deeper than she felt already. She hoped the farm wouldn't be too far from civilization if one could even consider the small town of Yreka civilized.

"Did you know I'm from Antwerp?" he asked her.

She nodded. "Oui, monsieur." Marrin prayed he wouldn't pressure her to say anything specific about the city—or any other part of Belgium, since she herself had never been there and Carina had told her very little about it. "I attended boarding school in Antwerp," she lied, saying exactly what Carina had coached her to say.

"Ah, Antwerp," he sighed. "The River Nete and St. Michael's Abbey. Have you been to the castle?"

What should she say? Think fast. "Oui." No, she mustn't lie about this. He might ask her for details. She tugged a windblown lock of hair from her mouth. "I mean, non, monsieur."

Mr. Stinson grunted. "Funny, I'd have thought the boarding school nuns would take you there. It's quite a famous site."

"I have seen it, but I never went to it, monsieur." She should stop lying now, or she'd get into trouble.

Mr. Stinson adjusted the reins and spoke gently to his horses before going on. "You won't find any boarding schools here. We have proper public schools in America, and you need to attend as soon as possible so you can learn English."

Marrin's heart thrilled. Attend school? She'd only dreamed of such an opportunity. A brisk wind kicked up, and she clapped a hand to her hat. "Where is the nearest school?"

The long hoot of a train whistle floated like a breeze through the air as he gestured behind them. "Not too far. On the outskirts of the south end of town. There's another school in Montague, the next town over, but the one in Yreka is closer. Do you know how to ride a horse?"

Her chest constricted, and she shook her head. "Non, monsieur." She'd always been afraid of the beasts and, with her distinct lack of coordination and balance, trying to ride would certainly result in calamity. But had Carina ridden horses? She'd never mentioned it.

"My ranch hand, George, will teach you to ride. Good, decent lad." Something about the kind way Mr. Stinson spoke of George caused her to cast him a sideways glance.

The ranch wasn't far from town and, after the hundreds of humble, lonely farmhouses she'd passed on her journey across the country, her heart leaped with a niggle of happiness as they passed through an arched wrought-iron gate scrolled with a circled "M" and the words "Greenwind Ranch." It was a fitting name, considering the blustery wind and lush fields grazed with horses and cattle, tucked into a small valley with a river winding like a ribbon through the middle.

Nestled amongst a stand of trees between two rolling hills was a Victorian house—a mansion grander than her aunt and uncle's villa in Amiens. It was so large, it would have been intimidating if it weren't for its cheerful and audaciously vibrant coral-pink siding trimmed with lacy white gingerbread and moss green shutters and gables. A stylish turret soared prominently above two chimneys, and a wide, wraparound porch beckoned to a sparkling blue pond with a view of Mt. Shasta to the south.

"Your Aunt Penelope wanted a pink house," Mr. Stinson said with a sad lilt to his voice. "I did it for her. She was such a merry soul. Wish you could have known her."

"Marie?" Marrin asked.

"Oh, I beg your pardon!" Mr. Stinson exclaimed. "I switched to English again. Merry is another word for jolly. Like heureuse." He chuckled and drew in a deep inhale.

"I wish I could have known Penelope," Marrin said with sincerity. "It's a lovely house. Like a tropical flower."

A stiffer breeze kicked up, and Mr. Stinson tightened the stampede string of his hat beneath his chin. "Home, sweet home," he said.

A young cowboy on horseback galloped over in a cloud of dust to meet them at the front steps to the house. He swung to the ground and ambled to the surrey, grabbing a bridle. "Howdy, Liam," he said, tapping the brim of his wide-brimmed hat to Marrin and linking his hazel-gray eyes with hers for just long enough to make her squirm and feel her cheeks flush pink. She dropped her head. The man was astonishingly good-looking.

Don't go falling in love with a hired hand, she commanded herself. She knew Carina had been expelled from boarding school for some sort of misconduct. Something about having a saucy attitude and defying school rules, as well as flirting with boys. Her fiancé was one of them. But Marrin didn't want that reputation and was determined to redeem Carina's tarnished image.

She also had to remember her new station in life. The real Carina Lejeune would never consort with a common, grungy cowhand.

"Ma'am?" asked a deep voice near her.

Marrin cast her gaze through lowered lashes and found the cowboy's hand hovering at her side, palm-up. Heart pounding ridiculously, she placed her fingers in his rough, calloused palm and quivered at the weakness that shot up her arm. Before she realized what was happening, his hands closed around her waist—firm and startling. No man had ever touched her like that. Her breath caught, not from fear so much as shock. A hot rush flared through her as she lifted off the wagon, floating for a moment as though time slowed.

"Merci," she breathed as her feet found the ground. She slipped from his grasp and took an unsteady step back. A gust tugged at her skirt, and she clutched the fabric with trembling fingers to regain her balance.

It was the first time in her life she'd been that close to another young man her age, much less one so handsome.

"Carina, meet my lead ranch hand, George Royer," said Mr. Stinson in French. He switched to English and spoke to George. Marrin caught snippets of words, like Carina Lejeune, French, and English. "George was born in America," he said, speaking her language again, "but his grandparents are from Belgium, and he speaks some French. He's actually been there. Took him there myself several years ago to visit his grandparents." Marrin stiffened. Not again. She hoped it wouldn't come up in further conversation.

"It's a pleasure to meet you, Mademoiselle Lejeune," George said, his eyes twinkling, while one corner of his mouth tugged upward in his beard-scruffed face.

Her mind blanked, dipping into a neat curtsy. "Pleas— pleasure," she repeated softly, unsure if she'd said it right.

George's brow quirked, amusement flickering in his eyes. Beside him, Liam's mouth tightened just a fraction.

"Did they teach you that in boarding school?" George asked, a light snuff of a chuckle in his throat. "To curtsy like a maid?"

A confused heat burned her face. *Of course, they don't curtsy here,* she realized a heartbeat too late.

"My older sister was at Sint-Katelijne-Waver boarding school in Antwerp for a year. Is that where you attended?"

Marrin's throat squeezed. "Je ne comprends pas."

Liam translated, "He asks if you were forced to learn Flemish or Dutch, like his sister?"

"Non," she replied. "Tell him I only spoke French. I was taught a little Dutch, but I don't remember it." What was that Dutch phrase she'd heard? "Ik spreek niet goed Nederlands."

"Not bad," said Liam. "That's the one Dutch phrase I know, too."

Marrin let out her breath. *Please, no more talk about Belgium*, she prayed silently.

"So, you didn't study Flemish?" George asked in broken French. Marrin shook her head. "Lucky you. My sister said her Flemish teacher was a nightmare."

"I'm sorry to hear that," she said. "There were a few nightmare teachers there, actually." That was how Carina had described them, although she suspected the rebellious girl was more at fault than her teachers.

"Votre anglais...est..." George spluttered. "Oh, never mind. I can't speak French. I'm trying to say that your English is pretty good."

"Pretty?" The corners of Marrin's eyes crinkled. "Jolie bon?"

"It's a figure of speech," Liam explained before changing the subject and addressing George. "Carina needs to learn to ride a horse so she can get to and from school." Marrin's insides clenched. Not horses again. It was bad enough she had to learn to ride at all, but this handsome man was going to teach her? She'd fall and make a fool of herself, for sure.

"Can you find time in your schedule, George?" Mr. Stinson asked. "Maybe give your morning chores to that new cowhand?"

"Yes, sir," said George. "When does she start school?"

"The sooner, the better, before the term ends for the summer."

"Riding lessons tomorrow morning, then," said George, casting a half-smirk to Marrin.

Marrin pressed her lips together and nodded, dropping her head. What would she wear to ride a horse? Carina hadn't given her any riding attire.

"Your Aunt Penelope's riding clothes are still around somewhere," said Mr. Stinson, as though reading her mind. "Edith will find you something."

"Thank you, sir," said Marrin.

"Call me Uncle Liam."

"Yes, Uncle Liam," said Marrin. She turned to George. "And thank you, Monsieur Royer."

"You can call me George," said the cowboy, his deep, low voice sending flutters through her gut.

She looked questioningly at Mr. Stinson.

"It's all right, Carina," said Liam. "We're on more familiar terms here in America—especially out here in the west."

"All right then…George." Calling these two men by their first names felt ill-mannered. And, though George might be a lowly ranch hand, she could hardly wait for tomorrow morning and the chance to be with him again. Even if it meant having to ride a horse, she knew Carina would surely have felt the same.

CHAPTER 6:
Riding Lessons

"Travel is fatal to prejudice, bigotry, and narrow-mindedness." — *The Innocents Abroad*, Mark Twain (1869)

*S*and-eyed and stiff from days of train travel, Marrin slipped from bed, yawned, stretched, and tuned her ears to the sounds of clucking chickens, a rooster's incessant crowing, a barking dog, and birds. The songs of geese and a Grosbeak she recognized, but there was something else—a low moaning of something like… Were they foghorns? That made no sense out here far from any seashore.

She pattered to the window and pulled back the curtain to view a wide sky wisped with clouds. She unlatched the clasp and pushed up the window. The fresh, clean antiseptic aroma of junipers cleared her head instantly as she peered out at rolling grassy plains rimmed with mountains and green pastures dotted with lowing cattle. Ah, *cattle*. Those were the foghorns. She laughed at herself for being so obtuse.

Obtuse. Carina had taught her that word. Such an educated word. A smirk tugged at one corner of Marrin's lips. Back in France, she hadn't attended school since her parents died, but here, she was the niece of Mr. Liam

Stinson, a wealthy and respected rancher and landowner. She'd extract as much education as possible before she left this place. And, even if she got caught, education was something no one could take from her.

The breezes of the previous afternoon were replaced with a gentle stillness. She let the curtain fall and picked up an alarm clock from a desk beside the bed. She had little more than half an hour to take a quick sponge bath, dress, and scurry downstairs for her first day of riding lessons at five-thirty. Her heart drummed faster, and she smiled as George came to mind. She hugged her hands around her waist, where he had held her in his sturdy grip the day before.

Pulling on the late Aunt Penelope's loose, brown riding trousers, Marrin felt self-conscious and unladylike. What would George think? Would he find her pretty? She was being ridiculous. She had to stop thinking about him and focus. She braided and knotted a bun at the back of her head and settled a wisp of a curl alongside her cheek. If only she didn't have to ride a horse to be close to George Royer.

A waft of coffee and breakfast made her stomach growl. Descending the stairs, she tiptoed to the dining room, where she stumbled upon the hustle and clatter of half a dozen men coming and going. Another eight or so men sat crowded at a table, enjoying a quick and hearty breakfast of scrambled eggs, sausage, and freshly baked bread.

George was among the diners at the table. Hat off, his shock of blond hair and sandy beard were a contrast to his tanned skin. "Bon jour, mademoiselle," he called out. "You're up bright and early. Better get some food before the hoarders eat it all." He patted the empty space on the bench beside him. "Sit here, and we'll go over a few things before we begin your riding lesson."

She nodded and fought the warm dizziness that shot through her. She was to sit beside him at the table? So close? How would she concentrate on breakfast?

She braced herself for the onslaught of curious eyes as she made her way to the meal line.

"Get out of that line and come on in here to the kitchen, Miss Carina," said Edith, gesticulating. Marrin didn't understand many words, but she guessed at the invitation and bade the housekeeper and cook a good morning. "I see Penelope's clothes fit you fine," Edith noted. "You look like a genuine horsewoman." She handed Marrin a plate of food.

"Merci." Marrin gulped and took the plate, hoping she wouldn't trip and drop it all. And wondering if she'd ever come close to being a horsewoman.

"Now, if there's anything you don't understand in English, just ask George to translate. He's a good soul. He'll help you out." She gave Marrin a soft nudge toward the dining room.

As Marrin returned, carefully balancing her plate, a chorus of whoops and whistles erupted. One cowboy gave George a playful punch on the shoulder. Marrin blushed. They were probably teasing him because of her. Jutting her chin, she strode forward. The men parted, allowing her to take her seat beside George, acutely self-conscious of her trousers.

"Never mind them," George said in French. "They're a good, loyal bunch. You're safe with any of them. Liam wants us all to treat you normal, not like a princess."

Marrin hoped he wouldn't mention her trousers as she spread a napkin on her lap, just as Carina had taught her.

"Before you take a bite, let me caution you," George said. She shot him a wary glance. "You probably already do, but Uncle Liam likes us to say a prayer before meals."

"Of course," she mumbled.

She remembered Carina's sign of the cross gesture. Hand to right shoulder, then forehead. She tried this and fumbled before bowing her head. She whispered a quick prayer before picking up her fork. She tried to ignore the way George stared at her, but finally stopped, covered her mouth with a napkin, and ran her tongue over her teeth. Something must be wrong. Why else would he look at her like that?

"I'm not Catholic," said George, "but I've never seen the sign of the cross done quite like that before."

Marrin's cheeks went hot. "I converted to Protestantism," she whispered.

"Oh!" George laughed outright. "Most of us are Protestant too, so you don't have to pretend you're Catholic here."

Marrin let out a breath she didn't know she'd been holding.

"Have you ever ridden a horse before?" George asked, mixing English with French.

She shook her head. She'd been around horses back at her aunt and uncle's farm, but she'd never felt comfortable with them.

"Do you like horses?"

She lifted her shoulders in a shrug.

"I see. You're not afraid of them, are you?"

She loudly gulped a sip of coffee. "No, not afraid. Just a little nervous."

"Any particular reason? Did something happen to make you nervous?"

"No, they're just so big. They can step on you. Buck you off."

"A healthy fear, then."

"I suppose," she said, focusing on her meal, trying to mimic the way the other ranch hands ate.

"You don't have to eat like them to fit in," George remarked. "Just use the manners you learned in boarding school. That's what everyone expects of a lady."

Marrin froze, dropping her fork. Wiping her mouth with the back of her hand, she wondered what she was doing wrong. "I thought if I ate like them, they'd stop staring at me," she fibbed in a low voice.

"Non, mademoiselle," he snorted. "Quite the opposite. They stare more when you don't use the table etiquette expected of Liam Stinson's niece."

Marrin's entire face went hot. "Of course," she murmured. Despite Carina's scoldings, she still knew next to nothing of etiquette. She would have to observe George's manners carefully, since he seemed to know so much about them.

"I'm not hungry anymore," she admitted, giving up on the meal and placing her fork on her plate. "I think it's time for my riding lesson."

"That won't do either," George reprimanded. "Eat up, or you'll offend Edith."

He waited in silence as she shoveled eggs into her mouth and tried cutting her sausage with the side of her fork, causing it to slip and slide from her plate onto the table. She laughed as she retrieved it with her utensil and ate it like a lollipop.

A ranch hand across the table choked on his coffee, trying—and failing—not to laugh. Out of the corner of her eye, Marrin caught George looking at her askance, his brow slightly furrowed. Her stomach tightened. She must have broken another rule of etiquette, though she had no idea how. The other ranch hands were eating this way, so…why couldn't she?

"Stop watching me," she told George with her mouth full.

George shook his head and frowned. When she was finished, he pushed back his chair and stood, gathering her plate and utensils.

"Oh, I'll get those," she said, reaching for the plate and nearly knocking it from his grasp.

"Nope," he said, pulling them out of her reach. "I'll get your dishes this morning, but don't expect me to serve you every day." His eyes twinkled with mischief, and her heart melted again. Soon, his strong hands would be on her waist, lifting her onto a horse. Their hands would touch as he taught her to hold the reins. She could hardly wait.

George dropped the dishes off in the kitchen before leading Marrin across the barnyard to the stable. "This here is Pinto," he said in English, giving the horse a pat on the withers. Shafts of bright morning sunlight slashed through the dusty air. "He was Penelope's horse. An affectionate old soul."

Marrin brows puckered. "Affec--tion…?"

His hazel eyes felt as though they reached into hers, making her heart stumble. "Affectueux." The way he said the word made her gasp. She bit her lower lip and looked away, stepping boldly forward. She stumbled. Typical. She was always tripping over her own feet. A firm hand steadied her.

"Steady there, Sparky," George spoke French in a low voice that made her pulse gallop. "First, you need to properly introduce yourself. Speak softly. Treat him like a gentleman, and he'll treat you like a lady." His voice quieted.

Marrin's throat went dry. Was he toying with her? She flattened her lips into a thin line and reached out to pet Pinto's velvety nose. "That's it." George's tone was soft, encouraging.

They started by brushing and currying the horse. It wasn't bad, but as time passed, she grew impatient.

"Is this a riding lesson or just an excuse to get me to clean your horse for you?" she finally asked.

George grinned. "Who put a burr under your saddle, Sparky?"

"There's no burr. I just want to know when I'm going to do some actual riding."

"I thought you were afraid to ride."

She put a hand on one hip. "I never said I was scared. Just nervous."

George drew a long breath. "I want you and Pinto to

take your time getting to know one another before you progress to the next level of your relationship." She eyed George Royer with suspicion. Was he talking about horses? "See how sweet, gentle, and patient he is?" He ducked his head and mumbled, "You could learn a few things from him."

"I heard that," she shot back. His words stung a little. It wasn't the first time she'd been accused of being impatient.

"Brushing and currying a horse is essential before a ride. It removes any possible dirt, weeds, salty sweat, tangled hair, whatever. Anything lumpy that could cause irritation under his saddle and blanket."

"Like a burr?"

"Except we can't remove you, can we?" he said, eyes twinkling.

She felt her eyes kindle. "Are you calling me a burr?"

"Relax, Sparky."

"Why do you call me Sparky?"

He chuckled. "'Cause you're feisty and hot like sparks of fire." She gripped the brush tighter and bit down on a retort. Was that a compliment?

After brushing Pinto, George taught her how to pick stones from his hooves. Then came the saddling and bridling.

"How long is this lesson going to take?" she asked hesitantly.

"Hold your horses, Sparky. I'm just making sure you're comfortable being around Pinto."

"What does this mean: Hold your horses?"

He chuckled. "It means be patient."

"Oh," she huffed. Patience again.

"A horse always knows how you feel. If you're nervous or scared, he'll sense it, and you'll make him anxious. You don't want to go riding a tense and jumpy horse."

"Oh, I see," she said, smoothing a palm down Pinto's

smooth, sleek neck. He was placid and gentle, and he nuzzled her neck with his fuzzy nose. She inhaled, exhaled. Her heartbeat slowed; the nerves settled.

"Can you spare another twenty minutes?" George asked.

Her eyebrows spiked. "Don't you have to go back to work riding horses and roping cows and doing whatever cowboys do?"

"Cowboys?" He tossed her a smile full of mirth.

"Isn't that what you are?"

"Among other things, I suppose. I'll get to my riding and roping later." He chuckled. "Time to get you into the saddle."

Her knees jiggled. Oh, dear. On the ground, she was beginning to feel at ease around Pinto, but the horse was so tall. What if she fell? And with her lack of coordination, falling was a definite possibility.

"Place your left foot into the stirrup like this," George said, demonstrating. "Grab the saddle horn in your left hand and the back of the saddle with your right. Then pull yourself up to stand on one foot…" He rose and soared onto the horse's back. "…swinging your right leg over the horse, like so." He dismounted and stood at her side again. "Ready?"

"I suppose," she garbled. She placed her left foot in the high stirrup and bounced up three times, accomplishing nothing. Frustrated, she tried to pull her boot from the stirrup, but it stuck, and she lost her balance, twisting her ankle where it continued to hang. She yelped, and George caught her, steadying her with one strong hand firmly on her waist while he carefully, deftly dislodged her foot. She shoved him from her. As much as she liked the feel of his hands on her body, she didn't want him to get too comfortable touching her. She was his boss's niece, after all. He needed to remember his place. She would never be allowed to care for him in that way. Besides, she needed to work on ridding herself of Carina's bad reputation with men. If he hadn't heard about it yet, he would soon enough.

"Steady there, Sparky," he said. "I was only trying to help." He whistled. "I expected a relation to Mr. Stinson to be more agile."

She shot him a glowering pout. "No one ever said I was the nimblest person," she snapped.

"Or the most graceful," George said under his breath.

"I heard that."

"How old are you?" George asked, changing the subject.

"What an impertinent question."

"It just seems you've had plenty of time in your many years of life to learn to compensate for your lack of dexterity, and yet…"

It was true: There was no way to hide her clumsiness. She drew a deep breath and blew it out. "I guess it won't come as a surprise to you that I flunked out of ballet school."

The corners of his lips stretched upward. "You in ballet school," he muttered before speaking in a more instructional tone. "You just have to gain your balance and get a firm grip with your legs. You'll figure it out and start feeling at ease soon enough. Try again."

"I think I'm too short. Could I use a stool or something?"

"I'll boost you up this time, but you're not too short. You need to get a feel for the movement of pulling yourself up in one smooth motion."

She steadied her breath, placed her foot in the stirrup, grasped the saddle horn and saddle, and counted. She bounced and, on "three," she sprang upward and felt the firm, warmth of George's hands on her ribcage, lifting her.

"There, now. You did it," said George. He sounded almost proud.

"With your help." It felt good to be safely in the saddle, but she felt so precariously far from the safety of the ground.

"Don't forget to talk to Pinto and pet him. Give him some encouragement. Show him you're calm and relaxed."

"I'm *not* calm or relaxed." Marrin's throat was tight.

"Then pretend."

She forced a smile—for Pinto's sake and hers. "I feel like I might fall," she whispered.

"You won't. Just sit up straight and tighten your thighs. That's it. Let go of the saddle horn for a minute." She slid back her hands and let George unwind the reins from the horn. "Now give me your right hand." She held it palm up, and he placed the leather into it. "Hold it like so. Never wind it around your hand, or you could get tangled." He took her hand and paused to stroke the pads beneath her knuckles. Was he making advances or…? "Where'd you get these callouses?" he asked without meeting her eye.

She jerked back her hand. What lie could she invent this time? "Probably from…from…" She couldn't think of what to say, so she jabbed a heel into the horse's ribs, forcing the beast to lurch forward. "Whoa, whoa!" she cried, slipping sideways in the saddle and gripping the horn with both hands. She reached out and stroked the horse's neck and flicked a weak smile to George. "That made me a little jumpy."

"What about the callouses?" he prompted again.

She looked at her hands. "Oh, well… Don't you think you should look after your own onions?"

He chuckled. "Funny. Your uncle uses that same phrase. But, seriously, a refined young lady, such as yourself, shouldn't have callouses like those. What's your story?"

"It's…um…a little embarrassing and really none of your business, Mr. Royer," she said, her nerves trembling. "I…I got into a bit of trouble back at school, and the headmistress relegated me to working in the kitchen as punishment." She shot him a warning look. "Nothing too serious, I assure you." There was some truth to that. She'd spent a lot of time working in the kitchen and gardens back at her aunt and uncle's place—and Carina had gotten into trouble at school. She hated that George would wonder what crime she'd committed. What if Uncle Liam had already told him of Carina's sordid past? "I think the callouses will come in handy when it comes to riding."

"They will, actually," George agreed. He smirked. "Petite Mademoiselle Trublion."

"Please don't tell anyone," she begged. "I'm not really a troublemaker. It was a misunderstanding, and I'm trying to make a fresh start here."

"You're secret's safe with me."

She hoped she could trust him. Ironic, since she was the one lying through her teeth like a hypocrite.

"That should do it for today, Sparky," said George. "I'll help you dismount and show you how to untack."

"I'm afraid I won't be able to remember everything I've learned today, George."

"Not to worry. After you do the same thing day after day, it'll become routine." He instructed her, step-by-step, in how to dismount.

"But it's so far down." She hesitated, shivering.

"Don't worry. You won't fall. I've got you."

Was this the part where his hands would be around her waist again? She filled her lungs with air and slowly eased down with her foot.

"That's it."

The ground was a long way off, and the angle was awkward. She held onto the saddle as tightly as she could, but… "Oh, no," she muttered. "I feel like I'm going to fall."

"I won't let you fall," he promised.

All on her own and without his touching her, she allowed herself to slide slowly down, and her foot landed with a stumbling thud onto the floor of the stable. She was able to breathe again. But her left foot was still lodged in the stirrup, stuck in that same ungraceful position that had twisted her ankle earlier.

"Very good," he said. "You did it."

"Did I? My boot is stuck."

"You're fine," he reassured. The breath of his laughter was warm on the back of her neck. "Lean on the horse and keep a firm grip on the saddle while I help." Gently, deftly, he pulled her boot from the stirrup, eased her foot to the floor, then gave her a light pat on the back. "There you go. Back on solid ground. Easy as falling off a log."

"Easy as falling off a horse, you mean." Her legs felt like jelly.

"Mark Twain," he said.

"Mark what?"

"Mark Twain. He's an American humorist. He wrote the *easy as falling of a log* phrase in one of his novels. You probably won't read any of his work in school, but once you learn English, I highly recommend him."

"Mark Twain," she repeated. She flashed him a worried smile and pounded her thighs with her fists. "My legs are so shaky."

"Walk around, and you'll soon get your land legs back."

After a brief lesson in untacking the horse, he showed her how to hang everything uniformly and neatly in the tack room.

"Well, that's it for today, Sparky," he said. "We'll meet back here for another riding lesson tomorrow morning before church."

"It wasn't much of a riding lesson," she muttered.

"You'll be riding soon enough."

"What do you mean church?"

"Starts at ten o'clock and takes about half an hour to get there by buggy. You and Liam will go together. The rest of us take turns attending church every other Sunday. It's my Sunday to work."

"Oh." Church. Her stomach twisted with knots and

butterflies. This might be a chance to make new friends, but she feared what others might think of her. Would they look down on her as a foreigner, or would they treat her with respect as Liam's niece?

"Will there be a riding lesson every morning?" she asked George.

He brushed his hands together and turned his handsome face to hers again. "Every morning till you get comfortable on your own."

"Your Uncle Liam said to tell you he's out of town till tomorrow. He wants you to spend the rest of the day with Edith. She'll help get you settled and show you around the house. He expects you to meet him after your riding lesson tomorrow morning, before you leave for church." Alarm stabbed at her ribs. What did Liam want? "Don't look so worried, Sparky," George said with teasing eyes. "He's not your boarding school headmaster. He wants to show you around the property and get to know you better, is all."

"Oh." She relaxed.

"I'll see you tomorrow, mademoiselle," he said with a half-wink that prickled the hairs on her arms.

Heart thumping, she stammered out a curt "Au revoir" and spun round, making a quick pace to the house before she might make more of a fool of herself. Head bent, she smashed her lips together to suppress the grin that threatened to rip across her face and reveal her emotions to anyone nearby. The way this man spoke to her, looked at her, and touched her. Was he like this with everyone, or was he treating her specially? Would he ever try to steal a kiss? Would it be all right to kiss him? She pressed a cool palm to her hot cheek. Frightened as she was of horses, Pinto hadn't been too bad, and another riding lesson with George Royer could not come soon enough. Even though she really didn't like him for anything more than a friend. Or so she kept telling herself.

CHAPTER 7:
Greenwind Ranch

"Truth is stranger than fiction, but it is because Fiction is obliged to stick to possibilities; Truth isn't." — Mark Twain, *Following the Equator* (1897)

After another hurried, noisy breakfast and a riding lesson from George—still with no actual riding—Marrin shed her unflattering attire for a summery light blue frock with a lace-edged sailor collar. She couldn't help but smile as she wriggled her toes into a comfortable pair of low-heeled velvet slippers. Carina certainly had a flair for fashion. To stave off the spring chill in the air, Marrin shrugged on the fine linen traveling coat she'd stolen, and a fresh pang of guilt tremored through her. If it weren't for this coat, she might be an indentured servant today. On the other hand, if it weren't for the coat, she might not have started down a path of transgressions that were forcing her to commit lie after lie after lie.

She wondered about her future. What if Carina's parents came to visit and found her pretending to be their daughter? What did they want from her? Would they expect her to marry? Was Liam expecting that too? She needed advice, and the fact that Mr. Stinson had summoned her to his office might mean she could ask him some questions—

without revealing her true intentions, of course.

She trod lightly down the stairs and over a long, soft carpet that ran along the hall to Mr. Stinson's study. She tapped her knuckles on the door and held her breath, listening.

"Carina?" It was Mr. Stinson's deep voice.

"Oui, Uncle Liam."

"Come in," he said in French with a hint of gruffness. Marrin entered and gave a quick bob.

"Please dispense with the curtsies, Carina dear. The only maid I need around here is Edith," he scolded with a frown.

"I'm sorry," she apologized, wishing she could break her habit of curtsying.

"It's good you're dressed for church. Close the door a moment, please," said Liam. "I need to speak with you before our ride around the property this morning." Marrin complied and stood uncomfortably, hands clasped at her waist, lower lip pulled between her teeth.

"This is unpleasant business, but I need to speak with you about your conduct toward young men." Marrin's stomach clenched, and her breath sucked in so sharply, she nearly choked. "Your mother, my sister, told me some shocking things about your behavior involving risqué escapades with young men who visited you at Sint-Katelijne-Waver's boarding school. I don't want you consorting with any of my ranch hands. Especially not Mr. Royer." Marrin's temples tightened, and she fought back hot, angry fury. How dare Carina put her in this shameful position?!

"George is a good lad, and I won't allow you to break his heart. Do you understand?" Marrin nodded numbly. What risqué thing had Carina done to so thoroughly ruin her reputation? She dropped her head and longed to crawl out of the room. "Do I have your word that you won't flirt with or encourage George or any of my ranch hands?"

"Yes, sir," he mumbled, her cheeks flaming.

"The same goes for any young men at school, church, or anywhere else around here," he added.

Nearly bursting with outrage, Marrin jutted her chin and looked Mr. Stinson straight in the eye. "Uncle Liam, let me be perfectly clear with you. I did not do whatever you were told I did, and I am not the tarnished young woman you think I am. I was wrongly accused, I am completely innocent, and I will prove this to you through my good character, I promise you."

Liam Stinson's brows climbed his forehead. "Well, I'm glad to hear it, Carina. Your parents seem to believe the worst, but I'm prepared to give you the benefit of the doubt, as long as I don't see a single hint of shenanigans."

She wrinkled her brow and wondered about the word "shenani-something," but could guess its meaning. "I understand, Uncle. I am an honorable young lady. You'll see." She cringed at the falsehood in the confession as she smoothed sweating palms over the skirt of her stolen coat. She might be a liar and a thief, but she was no harlot. "And one more thing, Uncle Liam." His eyes glinted at her. "I have no interest in George Royer as anything more than an acquaintance. A friend, at the most."

Mr. Stinson stood, grunted a smile, and walked past Marrin. "I'm glad to hear it." Opening the door for her, he gestured for her to go on ahead of him. "I'm glad that's settled," he said as he followed her down the hall and onto the front porch.

Any fatherly advice Marrin thought she'd receive from Mr. Stinson was now gone forever, thanks to Carina and her escapades. Still fuming, she nearly tripped over a small black and white sheepdog that slept outside the door. Stepping around the dog, she looked up and froze as she clung to the handrail. George stood at the bottom of the steps, handsome and masculine as ever, his ill-behaved sand-ash hair blowing lightly in a breeze as he bent to kiss the nose of a horse. Marrin blinked, jerked her chin to clear her jumbled head, and proceeded on wobbly legs, praying she wouldn't trip as Jacques bounded past her down the steps.

George swung onto his horse, and Marrin climbed onto the wagon seat beside Liam. Jacques, the sheepdog, jumped into the wagon box and, with a light snap of the reins, they lurched forward, riding southward in the cool damp of morning past the pond. The massive grandeur of snow-capped Mt. Shasta loomed in the distance. Mr. Stinson pointed out his acres of land and its borders, indicating where far-off neighbors owned adjacent properties. With George's assistance of opening and closing gates, they drove alongside crops of green alfalfa hayfields and through rolling, green-grass hills where Liam's cattle roamed.

A rumble of thunder arose, and Liam pulled up on the reins. "Herd of wild horses," he said, flicking a finger in the direction of around twenty wild beasts pounding over the undulating plain, manes waving, hooves kicking up rocks and mud.

Marrin clutched the wagon seat, awestruck. Never had she seen anything like it. Enormous emerald plain, a rim of mountains, a vast expanse of blue, horses charging past on flying hooves that shook the ground and stirred a thick, aromatic bouquet of clay earth, wildflowers, and dew-dampened grass. She could barely swallow over the emotional knot in her throat. If only Robinette could see this. These animals were so free, so untamed, so confident and sure.

A tear wavered on the brink of spilling over. They were everything she wanted to be. She lifted a hand to shield her eyes and hide her face. She'd never be free here on this ranch in the middle of nowhere, living with Carina's ruined reputation, lying to everyone, pretending to be someone she wasn't. She had to take what little money she could scrape together and try to make it on her own. She had that tiny bit of money from Carina, but she'd need more. And she'd make her escape only after getting a chance to attend school. Nothing was more important than an education. She needed to learn to speak English and read and write before she could make it in this country.

A lone cry turned their attention from the vanishing herd, and George galloped off, twirling a lasso in the air and casting it expertly over a calf's neck.

"What is he doing?" Marrin asked, mesmerized by George's poise, balance, and athleticism.

"Rounding up a stray," said Liam.

"Where is he taking it?" asked Marrin.

"Back to its mother," Liam replied. "That reminds me—tell me about your mother, Carina."

Confusion suddenly crammed her brain. "Oh, um, I don't see Mother much. She sent me away to school and was always busy when I was home. I was raised by nannies and governesses, as you know, so…" It was everything Carina had told her to say, and she prayed Liam wouldn't ask more questions.

He snorted. "Sounds like Giselle. She was always selfish and vain." He paused. "I'm sorry to speak ill of your mother."

"It's all right. I was never close to her. In fact, I…I hardly knew her." It was the truth for both her and the real Carina.

"Back in Belgium, before I immigrated to America and married your Aunt Penelope, I was sweet on a girl. Gabrielle Dumont from Amiens, France." Marrin hiccupped a breath and held it, hoping Liam hadn't noticed. Her aunt and uncle had known the Dumont family. She'd even seen Mademoiselle Dumont on several occasions. She remembered her as a kind and beautiful lady with molasses-dark hair and melancholy blue eyes, but there were scandalous rumors about her being a divorcée and taking back her maiden name. "I asked Gabrielle to marry me," Liam went on. "We announced the engagement to our families and were immediately forbidden to marry. They said I was beneath her station." He shook his head. "That would never happen in the United States, where classes don't exist. Or is less existent, anyhow. Gabrielle returned to France, and I heard she married a short time later. I left for America with a broken heart and never looked back." He straightened on the wagon seat.

Marrin fought the longing to tell this man the truth—that Gabrielle was living in her hometown in Amiens and she was a spinster. The poor woman might still be in love with Liam. "How did you meet Aunt Penelope?" she asked, steering him away from thoughts of his lost love.

His lips curved a touch. "I met your Aunt Penelope at a hoedown." He laughed aloud at Marrin's quizzical look. "It's a country dance," he explained. "She was a spunky gal. Full of vim and vigor, folks said, although I always said she was full of piss and vinegar." He rounded an apologetic eye to Marrin. "Forgive my language."

"I would have liked Aunt Penelope," said Marrin.

"And she would have liked you."

"Why do you think so?"

"Penelope wasn't one to follow rules, and you are—or were—clearly a rule-breaker."

Marrin's cheeks flushed. "I broke a few rules, and I'm sorry for that, but let me remind you that I've never done anything improper with a man."

Liam smiled behind his mustache. "Penelope would have had a soft spot in her heart for you because of my troubled sister, Giselle."

"Why?"

"Carina, we both know Giselle wasn't a good mother to you and Alard. Penelope and I felt sorry for how she ignored you, leaving you to be raised by governesses, sending you off to boarding school so young. Penelope and

I loved children but sadly, we never had any of our own. Maybe now you understand why I was more than willing to take you in when Giselle asked me. Even though I had some doubts about your behavior, I thought this place might do you good. I hope it will. And I hope you'll make me proud to call you my niece."

"I may not be one-hundred percent honest and truthful, Uncle Liam, but I'm trying to be better," Marrin apologized.

He reached around and gave her an awkward pat on the shoulder. "We all need God's forgiveness, and I trust you're willing to turn over a new leaf." He lifted his arm stiffly from her and fidgeted with the reins as they watched George ride back to join them.

"New leaf?" Marrin asked.

Liam chuckled. "A fresh, new start in life," he explained.

"Yes," Marrin nodded, "that's exactly why I'm here."

Soon the threesome was on the move again, following a pair of wagon tracks through the grass.

"Penelope was a strong horsewoman," said Liam with a smirk. "She would have admired your natural balance and poise."

Marrin's eyes sparked at George. "Did he tell you I'm clumsy?"

"I never said that," said George, clearly eavesdropping.

Marrin glowered. "George still hasn't taught me to ride."

A chortle escaped Mr. Stinson's throat. "I think he's just a bit worried about your balance."

"Now you're calling me unbalanced?" Her voice was teasing.

"You said it, not me," said George.

Liam barked a chuckle, and Marrin relaxed. Surrounded by warm laughter, even if it was at her expense, she felt happy. She wanted these two men to like her. She found herself watching Liam's face for approval, craving some sign, however small, that he might come to see her as more than a burden or obligation. Maybe someday he'd even see her as a daughter. Silly and impossible, of course, but maybe she could make him proud. At the same time, she wanted to keep him from caring for her too much so his pain would be less if he ever found out the truth that a stranger lived in his home, taking advantage of his kindness, posing as his niece, playing on his affections, eating his food, wearing his late wife's clothes. Even riding Penelope's horse. He'd send her back to Virginia in a heartbeat.

"I'm eager to learn how to ride Pinto now that I'm less afraid him," said Marrin.

George's eyes danced. "Oui," he said. "*La Patience.*"

"I'm patient," she argued indignantly.

"I don't think so, Sparky," said George. "You're hotter than a firecracker and twice as jumpy."

Marrin cast a wary glance at Mr. Stinson. George's teasing was edging on flirtation.

"Your Aunt Penelope would have liked that fire in you," said Liam, "and so do I."

The compassion in Liam's words sucked the air from Marrin's chest, confusing her so completely that she sat stunned, wrapped in the generosity of the first real affection she'd felt since her parents died. And a mysterious ache in her soul threatened to make her cry for no apparent reason.

"Are you all right, Carina?" asked George.

"Of course," said Marrin, touching a finger to the corner of her eye to catch a tear.

Liam rested a smile on Marrin. "You're not crying, are you, my dear?"

"If I am, they're only tears of happiness, Uncle Liam," she replied.

That afternoon, Marrin sat on her bed, reading a book

on Belgian history she'd found in Uncle Liam's library. Yawning through pages of the Eighty Years' War, her mind wandered to church earlier that morning.

St. Mark's Episcopal Church, with its maize-gold exterior, oiled paper darkening the windows, arched vestibule doors, and interior rafters reminiscent of the hull of a ship, was charmingly picturesque in the midst of such a small, bustling country village.

Though she'd understood very little of the minister's message, the familiar strains of a hymn brought comfort. Following the service, people had greeted her with what felt like genuine kindness. Sadly, though, the few girls she met quickly abandoned her and skipped outside to talk and giggle in a small huddle. Marrin didn't blame them. How could they carry on a conversation with someone who didn't speak their language? At least they'd admired her dress. But she'd felt flashy and pretentious next to their modest calicos. She'd have to ask Liam if she could wear Penelope's more humble dresses and sunbonnets to school.

Funny how she'd come from humble means, had been thrust into a world of luxury, and now had to be humble again to fit in. Life was strange.

"Carina, supper!" Edith called from the foot of the stairs that evening.

"Coming," said Marrin, closing the bedroom door behind her and skipping lightly down the stairs to the first floor. Having spent a restful day perusing several of the books in Mr. Stinson's library and finding a very useful French-English dictionary, her stomach grumbled unexpectedly. Who knew reading Belgian history could work up an appetite?

Edith wrinkled her nose and opened the dining room door for Marrin, muttering something she didn't understand.

Mr. Stinson and George both stood as she bobbed a quick curtsy. Blast! Why did she keep doing that? George made little attempt to quell a grin, and she froze. Why was George at the dinner table?

"Welcome, little maid," said Liam, chuffing lightly.

"Bonsoir," she greeted, forcing her legs to move. Mr. Stinson pulled out a chair for her, and she'd barely seated herself before he spread a napkin on his lap and said a prayer. Marrin vowed to copy everything he did to keep from making a fool of herself.

A quick second after saying his "Amen," Liam squinted at her. "Did you not have time to change before dinner, Carina?"

Marrin's head went hot. Had she broken another rule of etiquette? "Oh, I lost track of time and didn't want to be late," she said defensively before adding, "I'm sorry, Uncle Liam. It won't happen again." She noticed that both George and Liam were dressed in nicer, cleaner clothes. Was she supposed to change clothes before every meal? Why? And what should she wear?

She was careful to copy every move that Liam and George made during their soup course, while she continued to wonder about his presence there. He must be more than a ranch hand to Mr. Stinson. Both men slowly dipped their spoons away from them before drawing them to their mouths. Odd. It wasn't the way she'd ever eaten soup before, but she'd make the best of it. She slurped a drop and clattered her spoon into the bowl.

"Pardonnez-moi," she said, dabbing her lips with a napkin.

"It's a little hot," George commented.

"If you think I'm clumsy with my soup, you should see me around horses. Oh, that's right, you have." There was a snicker from George.

"Carina, there's something that puzzles me," said Liam. "If you know all the rules of etiquette that you learned in boarding school, why do you not always follow them?"

Marrin's insides turned to jelly. "Um, yes, about that." She fought to buy time and find some plausible excuse. "I do apologize. The fact is, I…" What could she say that would be at least half true? She couldn't keep on with all this lying. She was beginning to lose track of what was real and what she'd invented. A muddy story surfaced in her mind. "I was definitely taught, but I was such a rebellious little urchin, I refused to follow rules, and the truth is I forgot a lot of things." She placed her hands on the table on either side of her soup bowl. "Would you mind refreshing my memory?"

George's cheeks flushed in his tanned face, and Liam's eyes registered a hint of alarm.

"I suppose so," George said uncertainly.

"You're a puzzle, Carina," said Mr. Stinson, dabbing at his mouth with a napkin. "You curtsy like a common servant, don't dress for supper, and eat like a cowhand."

"I'm terribly sorry that I keep making mistakes. I want to learn to do the right thing," she said, her voice pleading.

"How was your education in boarding school?" Liam asked, causing Marrin's gut to cave in.

"Please don't ask, Uncle Liam," she begged, searching frantically for a way out of the interrogation that might ensue. "You know I didn't do well in school." She gulped draughts of water to stave off the mounting pressure.

"In what year did Belgium's declaration of independence from the Netherlands take place?" asked Mr. Stinson.

She'd been reading about Belgian history, but she feared making a mistake, so she feigned choking on a swallow of water. Was Mr. Stinson testing her? "Fifty or sixty years ago?" she guessed tentatively. "I never was good at remembering dates."

"Close," said Liam gruffly. Marrin wriggled. Why was he distrusting her?

"It was 1830," she said, attempting to breathe over the lump of sawdust in her throat. Was that correct? She watched Liam touch a glass of wine to his lips.

"Correct," he said presently, replacing his glass on the table. "History and politics." He eyed her again. "Our dear King Leopold is married to whom? And what country is she from?" Marrin looked down, toying with the napkin in her lap. "Carina?" he prompted again.

"Yes, Uncle?" She barely dared to peer up at him. Her stomach clenched like gripping claws, and she pressed hard on her knees to keep them from shaking, fighting to keep her secrets from spilling like soup from a broken bowl. She was familiar with the monarch of France, so…

"Is it Princess Margherita of Austria?" she asked, twisting her napkin into a rope on her lap. "Or, no, Princess Margherita is the queen of France, isn't she? Oh, dear. I'm afraid I've never been very good at answering questions under pressure. I panic, and my mind goes blank." Nothing false about that.

"Princess Margherita is indeed the queen of France," said Liam, "but the female reigning monarch of Belgium is Princess Marie-Henriette of Austria." He tore a chunk from his slice of bread and mopped it across his dinner plate. "What's the latest news of your brother, Carina?"

Marrin's stomach growled, and she drew an unsteady breath, wondering why he was peppering her with so many questions. And what was Carina's brother's name again? Aaron?

"Aaron," she began, stopping herself. But, no, it wasn't Aaron. What was it? She coughed and tapped her chest. "Excuse me. Um." Oh, yes! Alard!

"You're asking about Alard?"

"That's right," said Mr. Stinson.

"Yes, well, he's a dastardly beast," she said, rolling her eyes. "We never got along. You know how brothers and sisters can be."

Liam nodded and pushed back his plate as Edith entered, setting dessert plates before each of them.

"Oh, no, thank you, Edith. I couldn't possibly eat another bite," said Marrin, welcoming the chance to collect her thoughts. "Dinner was delicious, Edith," she added in French. She made an attempt at English. "Thank you, Edith. You are a good cooker." Edith chuckled, glanced at Marrin's plate, and frowned.

"You've hardly touched your food, Mademoiselle Carina."

Marrin touched her stomach. "I'm so full, I couldn't eat another bite." Another lie. She was, in fact, still very hungry.

Edith scolded Marrin for not eating enough as she gathered the dishes and departed. At the same time, Marrin tried to remember Carina's description of her brother.

She felt George's eyes on her. "You are a good cook," he said.

"What?" Marrin startled. "How do you know that I cook?"

He laughed. "No, I mean you don't say *cooker*, you say *cook*. Edith is a good cook."

"Oh, I see," she blushed.

"Back to your brother, Carina," said Mr. Stinson as he cut into a slice of dessert.

"Alard left home several years ago and never wrote to any of us," said Marrin. "He moved to America, in fact. He lives on the East Coast somewhere, last we all heard."

"What's so dastardly about him?" asked Liam between bites of what looked like raspberry clafoutis. If Marrin weren't so stressed, she would have enjoyed eating such a delectable treat.

"He's a selfish beast," she answered, careful to describe him exactly as Carina had done. "He cares for no one but himself." There. Nearly word-for-word.

"Selfish like…" Liam shook his head. "Never mind,"

he muttered.

"Like my mother?" Marrin inquired daringly with the hope of diverting Mr. Stinson from his interrogation.

"I'm sorry. I shouldn't have said anything."

"My mother is selfish," she said, allowing her voice to tremble as she untwisted her napkin. "She never cared much for Alard or me."

Liam shifted in his seat. "I'm sorry for that, Carina."

George's eyes widened uncomfortably.

"It's all right," Marrin replied. "I think it has made me stronger and more independent. Or, as some people might say, stubborn and headstrong." She lifted her eyes to George.

"Definitely that, Sparky." George winked and, though it meant absolutely nothing, it quickened Marrin's pulse. She shot a glance at Uncle Stinson, hoping he'd missed the gesture. He might scold her for it and think she'd done something to encourage him. But he wasn't looking. Thankfully.

She changed the subject. "Uncle Liam, George still won't let me ride Pinto. All he does is lecture me and make me brush and curry that horse till my arms nearly fall off."

Liam's mustache tugged down at the corners. "She's got to learn to ride so she can go to school, George. I thought she'd be ready for school tomorrow morning."

"Well, Liam," said George, clearing his throat. "There's just a certain matter of coordination."

"Oh, please," Marrin pouted. "I'm not that bad." She watched George's lips press together.

"George is a fine horseman, and I trust his judgment, Carina. However…" He turned a playfully stern face to George. "…the sooner my niece learns to ride, the sooner she can get back to her education. Summer's about to start, and I want her to get at least a week or two of schooling in before the end of the term. Give her another riding lesson tomorrow, but make sure she's ready to ride to school by

Tuesday. Or Wednesday at the latest. Understood?"

George nodded curtly. "Understood, sir."

"I can hardly wait to attend school," said Marrin without thinking.

"I thought you hated school," said Liam.

"Oh," Marrin licked her lips. "That was boarding school with all the annoying nuns. I'm looking forward to school here, meeting new people, making new friends, and learning about America."

Mr. Stinson cast her a suspicious look before addressing George.

"How did you convert from Catholicism to Protestantism?" he asked.

She hoped she did a fairly decent job of explaining that she'd converted when a friend from school invited her to church one time during a holiday break.

After that, the men's conversation reverted to English, leaving her out of the conversation. Relieved to finally have the focus off of her, she sipped her glass of water with a shaking hand, while discreetly watching George and Liam. George leaned and rocked back in his chair, his muscular chest tight beneath his shirt. If she wasn't careful, she might allow her gaze to linger too long on his physique and handsome face. Mr. Stinson would disapprove.

She averted her eyes and toyed with her napkin as questions crowded her mind. Why was George so casual with Mr. Stinson? Were the two related? Why else would he be invited to dine at the ranch owner's table?

George caught her eye, and her heartbeat quickened. She looked down at her lap, squeezing her lips in a bid to remove the blush that had immediately spiked the temperature in her cheeks. The way he looked at her sometimes was… She didn't know how to describe it. She couldn't allow herself to feel anything for him. Not even infatuation.

Mr. Stinson was no fool, and, with her clumsiness, lack

of manners, academic ignorance, and errors concerning Belgian history and politics, Liam's suspicions were obviously roused. If she kept making mistakes, he'd confront her, and she'd be forced to tell him the truth. And that meant slavery and probably never seeing her sister again. She had to write to Carina and put together an emergency exit plan. Just in case the worst should happen.

CHAPTER 8:
Balancing Act

"All you need in this life is ignorance and confidence, and then success is sure." — Mark Twain, *Notebook* (1898)

*M*arrin stood, stretched, and pushed back the ruffled white curtains framing the window of her bedroom. In the light of a new morning, Mr. Stinson's seeming mistrust of the previous evening suddenly felt long ago and far away. Probably only imagined. Surely, he couldn't have meant to test or trap her. She shook away any residual spasms of dread and splashed her face with water before pinning up her mess of curls and pulling on Penelope's riding trousers. She was probably taking things too seriously, but she should be more careful.

Forehead puckering, she clucked her tongue at the frumpy image reflected in the tall mirror. If she ever tried to find a husband, she'd be a dismal failure. Thankfully, this was not her goal. Not yet. "She was here to learn to ride a horse and get an education. She also needed to figure out a way to eventually leave Mr. Stinson and his ranch to make it on her own—so she could reunite with her little sister."

Robinette. She wanted to send her a letter, but how could she do that? Even if a letter reached her, what would keep her aunt and uncle from intercepting it and discovering

Marrin's whereabouts? The thought clamped around her lungs tighter than a corset. No, the letter would have to be delivered directly into Robinette's hands. Carina was likely in France by now. Maybe she would be willing to help her.

At breakfast, tearing at a slice of freshly baked sourdough bread with her teeth, Marrin sat on a chair in the kitchen, where she wouldn't be teased or corrected by George for her poor manners. As she watched Edith splash sudsy water on the dishes in the washbasin, guilt clutched at her gut. She was accustomed to service and should be helping Edith, not pretending to be Mr. Stinson's well-to-do niece. She knew next to nothing about rich people and how to behave like one, but she had to admit it was kind of nice to be waited on.

"What to plan for tomorrow's meals?" Edith asked herself aloud. "I wonder if I have enough beef and cabbage to make…"

Marrin almost spoke up with a menu suggestion, but stopped herself in time. It would never do for her to reveal that she knew her way around a kitchen. She missed cooking. Not that Edith wasn't good—she was excellent—but it would be fun to share her own expertise in the kitchen. Liam and George might appreciate Marrin's pâté de canard d'Amiens or flamiche aux poireaux. Or her baguettes baked with freshly-ground flour, slathered with churned butter from Monsieur Gagneux's dairy…

A deluge of homesickness constricted Marrin's throat, and a bite of bread caught in her windpipe. "Excusez moi," she apologized in answer to Edith's concerned expression. Eyes watering, she took the glass of water Edith handed to her. Funny how thoughts of ordinary bread and butter could make her miss home.

She bit off another piece of bread and chewed, her hunger finally staved. She didn't want to worry herself or make something out of nothing, but she had to ask Carina what to do about Uncle Stinson's suspicions. What if he voiced his concerns to Carina's parents? What if they found Carina in Brussels? Carina's parents would immediately wire Mr. Stinson and expose Marrin as the imposter she was. She had to write to Carina soon. They needed a better plan.

"Mademoiselle Carina?" a male voice pierced her thoughts, and her lashes fluttered in confusion. "Where in the world are you?" George asked, a slight tease on one corner of his mouth. "I had to say your name three times."

"Je suis désolé," she answered. "I'm sorry. I was thinking of home. A little homesick, I suppose." *She had to get used to being called Carina!*

"All this is quite a change for you, I imagine," he said, a hint of sympathy in his expression. "Are you ready to ride?"

She stood, nodded, and handed her plate to Edith. "So ready," she said with a nervous twitch at the corner of her mouth as she attempted to sound more confident than she really was.

As they left the kitchen, George said something to Edith that made the housekeeper blush and respond with a boisterous retort. George held the back door open for Marrin, and she swept past him onto the wraparound porch, sensing the subtle touch of his hand as it hovered over the small of her back. Her body prickled at the sensation, but she went to the steps, determined to make it clear to him that she was no flirt.

Her foot twisted in her descent on the stairs. "Whoa, there, Sparky," said George, jutting out a hand to steady her. "You sure you haven't been hittin' the cognac this morning?" Marrin understood enough of his stilted French and pitched him a disapproving glance. Blast her clumsiness! And what a mistake to look him in the eye! George Royer was more handsome than ever, if that was possible. Her breath caught as he kept a light hold on her arm, the warmth of his touch seeping into her skin like a fever that muddled her thoughts.

She tossed her head and forced herself to concentrate on her feet. Though she was wary of Liam possibly catching her in a questionable position with George, she couldn't help but savor the moment. His closeness was like a syrup-soaked bite of Amiens Savarin with Chantilly cream—sweet, warm, and…tempting.

After successfully passing a tacking and saddling test, Marrin received a flash-dimple of approval from George before his firm grip boosted her into Pinto's saddle, and the solid strength of his hands on her waist dissolved her insides to a state of near-paralysis.

"Thank you," she muttered, both embarrassed and exhilarated by her body's reaction to him. Despite wearing Aunt Penelope's trousers, her feminine décolleté had clearly caught George's attention—his face flushed, and he cast a confused glance at Pinto's bridle.

"I won't lie," George said, tightening his grip on Pinto's reins. "I'm a little nervous about teaching someone else to ride. Horses can be unpredictable."

The horse shifted beneath her, and Marrin slipped precariously to one side. "Oh, non!" she yelped, her fingers tightening on the saddle horn.

"Don't worry. You won't fall," said George, hooking his arm about her waist. "Find your balance and sit up straight." Marrin shifted to the center, lifting her chin and feeling the burn of George's hand on her back.

"Hold Pinto's lead just like this… wait, maybe a bit tighter," he muttered, tension creeping into his jaw. He adjusted Marrin's stirrups twice, frowning slightly as if trying to anticipate any sudden movement from the horse.

Marrin noticed the slight crease in his brow and the tension in his jaw. Somehow, it made her trust him even more.

"Good," he said. "Ready to do some real riding?" She nodded. "Give your legs a little squeeze and let go. It'll set Pinto to walking." She did as she was told, and the horse stepped forward.

George led them out of the barn to a round pen, where he taught Marrin more about the intricacies of riding. She found it gratifying to finally learn to mount and dismount on her own, and she began to ride without George's assistance.

"You're doing well, mademoiselle," he replied, his eyes glinting with the hint of a smile—and a little pride.

Things were going well, and Marrin was beginning to feel comfortable with her newfound ability to remain in the saddle and not make a fool of herself. Attempting a posting trot was where things began to go wrong, however. Her lack of coordination kept her from capturing a rhythm, which meant she was soon suffering from jarred lower back and hips, bruised buttocks, and a loss of all strength in her thighs. Finally, body suffering, she begged to quit for the day. "I'm so sore," she pouted.

"Not as sore as you'll be tomorrow," George said with a snuffle. "I recommend soaking in a hot bath and rubbing some Watkins Liniment into those twig arms and legs of yours."

"Twig?" she asked.

He translated the word into French: "brindille," and she dropped her jaw. She would have protested, but he didn't let her get a word in. "Congratulations, though. You just finished a full two hours of riding and did remarkably well, Mademoiselle Lejeune."

"Merci," Marrin returned with a gust of exhaustion. She twisted to drop down from the saddle and limped stiffly to Pinto's head. She stroked his cheek and thanked him for a good ride.

"Walking to school would take you a good two hours, but on horseback, you'll make it in about forty minutes."

"And I'll be ready for a nap by the time school starts," said Marrin, rubbing her back and stretching her legs in awkward poses whenever George wasn't looking. "Will I always be this achy?"

"Your body will adjust after about a week of steady riding."

"It will take a week?" Marrin practically yelped.

George chuckled. "Yup." He took Pinto's lead rope and turned toward the barn.

"I need to sit," she huffed.

"Oh, no, Sparky, I'm not letting you off that easy. Before you relax, you need to unsaddle and untack Pinto. I have to make sure you can do all this on your own before and after school every day."

"Can I leave the saddle on Pinto while I'm at school?" she asked.

"Nope," he stated firmly.

She sighed. "When will I be able to ride to school?"

"Tomorrow."

"Tomorrow? Wonderful!" she exclaimed. "But that means I'll be in utter aching pain every day of my first week of school!"

"We'll leave early so you'll have plenty of time to take breaks and stretch your legs along the way."

"We? You're going with me?"

"Yes. And, if anything goes wrong, we can turn back, and I'll take you in Liam's surrey."

"What do you mean by anything going wrong?" she asked with worry in her words.

His shoulders jiggled up and down. "I just mean if you're too sore and tired."

Marrin tightened her jaw. "I'll be fine. I want to attend school." At last, she'd experience some real freedom and independence. She could explore the town of Yreka, too—and maybe even find a part-time job. "Did you attend school, George?" She began unbuckling the straps of the horse's girth.

"Went to the same school you'll be going to. Graduated three years back. You'll like the schoolmaster, Miss Trimble. She's a good teacher. A bit strict." Marrin's eyes widened as she lifted the saddle and stumbled sideways, nearly falling into the barn wall.

"You sure Edith didn't spike your coffee this morning, Sparky?" George asked with a smirk.

"Very funny," she retorted, taking a deep breath and readjusting herself as she lugged the heavy saddle to the tack room. She was strong and accustomed to lifting heavy buckets of coal and water back home in Amiens, but her physical strength didn't make her any less clumsy.

"Sparky, I do declare you are a disaster waiting to happen," said George.

"You have no idea," she said under her breath as she plopped the saddle onto its rack and

slapped her hands together before wiping dust and grime on her trousers. "How is Miss Trimble strict?" she asked.

"Don't worry about her," said George. He paused, as if reconsidering. "Just remember these rules: Don't be late, don't roll your eyes at her, don't speak out of turn. Oh, and don't chew and spit tobacco anywhere within a mile of the schoolhouse. Stick to the rules, and you'll be fine."

"I guess my chewing tobacco habit will have to end," said Marrin.

George snorted as the two removed more tack from the horse and carried it to the tack room.

"What does rolling eyes mean?" she asked George.

He explained with animated demonstrations that made her laugh.

"Did you chew tobacco, George?" she asked.

"Nope, but other boys tried to and got suspended from school. The worst thing I ever did was show up tardy a couple of times. She made me stand in the corner with a dunce cap on my head. I suggest you leave home half an hour early to avoid that fate.”

“What is a dunce cap?” she asked.

“A silly, tall, pointed paper hat that teachers put on students to humiliate them when they do something wrong.”

“Does the teacher often make students wear the dunce cap?” Marrin asked with apprehension creeping into her voice.

“Don’t worry, Mademoiselle Carina,” said George, handing her a brush. “Miss Trimble will be more lenient with you, since you don’t speak much English.”

“Lenient?” she asked, brushing Pinto alongside George as he did his best to explain in French what the word meant.

“Ah, I see,” she said, attempting to speak in English. “I hope she will be patient with my bad English. Will she not like me because I am a stranger?”

A smile quirked on his lips. “I think the word you’re looking for is *foreigner*.”

“Yes, foreigner,” she said.

“Miss Trimble doesn’t dislike foreigners,” George said slowly, “but she’ll expect you to learn English as quickly as possible.”

“Oh, dear,” Marrin groaned.

“But have you noticed that I speak less and less French and more and more English to you every day?”

“I suppose you’re right,” she said, clamping down on a smile. She didn’t want to be too proud of herself. “I am understanding more each day, but I’m afraid of making a fool of myself.”

“You do that just by walking,” he said.

“What if I ever have to throw or catch a ball?” Marrin asked uneasily as they finished up with Pinto’s brushing. “Balls and I don’t get along. I always duck when I see one coming. She will make me wear the dunce hat.”

George laughed outright. “Not for that, she won’t. I don’t think she can punish you for being gangly and awkward."

"Like a twig?" she asked.

"Exactly," said George. "The worst Miss Trimble will do is send you inside to read books."

She perked up. "Does Miss Trimble have many books?" She wanted to read and learn as much as possible about everything.

"She has loads of books," said George, nodding. He picked up a bucket of brushes and returned to the tack room with Marrin following close behind. "Plus, there's a library in town if you want to read more. And your uncle has quite a few books as well."

"Yes, I've tried reading some of them," she said.

A smile softened George's lips. "Are you a secret bookworm?"

"What is bookworm?" she asked. George explained. "Ah. Peut être," she responded. "Maybe."

"You're a mystery, Mademoiselle Carina," he said. "For a girl who had to be sent all the way to America because she got into some sort of mischief at her boarding school in Antwerp, you don't strike me as a troublemaker."

The air in her throat caught for a split second before she regained composure. "What have you heard about me?" she demanded, knowing her face had pinked.

"Don't worry, Sparky. Liam only told me you got into some trouble at your school and you're here to make a fresh start."

"I'm a twig turning over a new leaf," she said, chuckling at her own joke.

George rolled his head and eyes wildly.

"You have no idea how much trouble I can be, Monsieur George Royer," Marrin said, realizing too late that her words might sound coy. She cleared her throat and coughed. "What I mean is that I did rebel against some school rules, but I was misunderstood and falsely accused. I'm trying to reform myself into a charming, graceful, educated young lady.”

"You're still a mystery," he said, his face clouding.

"You are too," she said, indignant.

"Me, mysterious? Never," said George. "I'm an open book."

"I enjoy books," Marrin said. She looked away and shook her head as she patted Pinto on the rump. She shouldn't have said that. She'd meant it to be coy, and that was wrong of her.

George's eyes narrowed to slits. "Are you flirting with me, Mademoiselle Carina?" His voice was rough.

Heat churned within her. "I don't understand," she said, hoping a lie would cover her mistake.

"I think you know exactly what you're doing, mademoiselle. But, for your information," said George, sucking in his cheeks before he spoke again, "I, too, enjoy reading, and you, Miss Carina, are a beguilingly closed book that I'd like to read."

Marrin cleared her throat and felt her face flush. "No flirting," she commanded in French. "Uncle Stinson forbids it."

"I wouldn't dare," said George with a wink and a tip of his hat. "Have a nice day, Sparky."

"I am serious, George," she shot back at him as he walked away.

"Yes, ma'am," he called over his shoulder, giving her a quick saluting wave. "I am too."

CHAPTER 9:
The Letter

'I didn't have time to *write* a short *letter*, so I wrote a long one instead.' –Mark Twain

*A*fter washing her hair and soaking in a hot bath that offered some solace to her aching body, Marrin sat at the desk in her bedroom. She dipped a feathered pen in ink, blotted the tip, and hovered the pen over a sheet of clean paper. She was waiting for some sort of organization to form in her head. Her eyes stared northward out the window. The Shasta River's ribbon of silver blinked and sparkled amongst the rolling hills, and beautiful white-capped periwinkle mountains stitched a jagged line on the distant horizon. It was time to devise a plan.

Setting pen to paper, she scribbled some thoughts: Ask Miss Trimble for summer lessons and books, ask Uncle Liam for books to read, ask if I can work in town or on the ranch….

She paused. What excuse might Carina come up with for wanting to earn money? New dresses? New shoes? A horse of her own? A wagon? No, Uncle Liam would probably buy her clothes and lend her a horse and wagon.

Money to return to Belgium? Carina's parents would likely send money for that, but they'd send it to Liam, and he'd buy the railway and steamship tickets.

She dipped and blotted her pen again before scratching out the words, "June 1895." It was a year from now. With hard work, she might be able to graduate in that short time period—especially if she was able to get a head start on her education over the summer. Also, over the next twelve months, she'd need enough money to make her escape and return to France for Robinette.

She listed various items and estimated costs for her travel needs: Stage, train, food, lodging—and a bedroll and pillow, in case she was ever on her own without a hotel. She shuddered at the thought. Overwhelmed, she crumpled the paper and tossed it into a wastebasket. How and where could she earn enough? Carina's small pittance was only a start. Working in town was her best option. She'd try to find a job and work a few hours after school each day—and during the summer months. She couldn't tell Liam.

A breeze slid through the window and caught the stationery paper. She slapped a hand on it and groaned. "Ugh!" She couldn't play the role of Liam's niece and be his servant at the same time. That was her old life. What would the real Carina do? If only she could make herself think like her. If Carina wanted to be independent and earn her own money by working in town, what action would she take?

Her eye caught Jacques, the sheepdog, ambling across the yard. As he disappeared into the barn, she turned her attention to formulating a letter to Carina. How was her fiancé—or new husband? How was married life? Where was she living now? She went on to inform Carina of all that had transpired in California at Greenwind Ranch with Mr. Stinson, then, praying it wouldn't be the case, asked if Carina had made any contact with her own parents in Belgium.

She paused, pen dangling. How could she ask Carina to deliver a letter to her sister in France? The journey was long, and Carina couldn't risk running into Marrin's aunt and uncle herself. She and Carina looked too much alike!

It was asking the world, but maybe Carina's new husband would be willing to deliver the letter to Robinette. Surely, he had reason to travel to Paris now and again. Perhaps he could stop off in Amiens on the way there and drop it off. Yes, that would work. She ended her letter with an emphatic warning that the contents of her letter to Robinette were highly confidential and must never fall into the wrong hands.

Upon signing off with a salutation, Marrin set aside the papers to dry and spread a new sheet of stationery upon the desktop. Dipping the pen again, she tapped the ink blotter and crafted a letter to Robinette, surprised at the sudden emotion that swept onto the page as she told her little sister how much she missed her, along with news of all that had transpired on the ship across the Atlantic, the train ride across America, and her new life and adventures in California.

She promised she'd return to France again for her. Someday, the two of them could be sisters again.

CHAPTER 10:
School

"Kindness is a language which the deaf can hear, and the blind can see." Mark Twain — Attributed to *Notebook* writings, c. 1898

Marrin would never admit it to George, but every muscle in her body felt as stiff and tight as piano wires. Still, she managed to tack Pinto on her own with minimal groaning and almost no help from George, which gratified her to the bone.

In the clean, damp freshness of a rain-washed Wednesday morning, Marrin strapped her tin lunch pail to the saddle and mounted, riding out at seven o'clock down a narrow trail that cut a shorter path to town than the dusty wagon road. There would be plenty of time to make the trek to the schoolhouse, where classes began at nine. The only difference about this morning's ride was Marrin's attire. She wore one of Aunt Penelope's plain calico dresses and a pink gingham sunbonnet. Though the ensemble wasn't nearly as fashionable as anything Carina had given her, it was certainly more feminine than trousers, and she knew she'd fit in with the other girls at school. The trouble was, Marrin was unaccustomed to riding in a skirt, and the extra fabric wadded up at her waist made her riding even less graceful.

It was difficult to find the saddle horn and, when Pinto took a gallop through a muddy, wooded ravine, lunging up the opposite side, she began to lose her balance, slipping precariously as she leaned forward and grabbed the horse's neck, wrapping her fists in his mane.

"Hold on," George called out from behind her.

She held on but was unable to correct her seat. Like a slow-moving dream, she fell sluggishly in a maladroit tumble that landed her on her backside in a scree of gravel, her skirts flying into her face as she slid into a puddle. Pushing her skirt from her face, she thrust the fabric over her legs to cover the petticoat and bloomers that had been indelicately on display to George.

Embarrassment burned her face as she propped one hand in the wet mud, finally managing to sit up. And then there was George, suddenly squatting at her side, his hand extended, palm-up. "Are you all right?" he asked, his granite-hazel eyes wide with concern.

She tightened her lips and hesitated before placing her hand in his. "So, this is why we left early," she said, "so there'd be plenty of time for Marr—Carina—to make a fool of herself on the way to school." She rose, stepped gingerly out of the puddle, and allowed George to steady her before she jerked herself free of him. Wiping her hands on her skirt, she thanked God she hadn't accidentally revealed her real name to him.

"You sure you're not hurt, Sparky?" There was no humor in his words.

"I'm fine. No broken bones." She shook out her skirt and used a rock to scrape mud from her boots. "I apologize for my lack of modesty and deplorable lack of coordination."

"You've muddied your skirt," said George, frowning.

"I'll be fine." It was true, but she had some safety pins and other emergency provisions in her saddlebag for just such an occasion.

"Miss Trimble doesn't take kindly to students who arrive at school dirty," George warned.

"I'll be fine," she answered pertly.

"Let me walk you and your horse up the hill," he said, offering his hand again. "It's steep, and there's no need for you to go falling again." She didn't want to give in to his assistance but acquiesced. This was no time for an argument. "Who's Marr-Carina?" he questioned in a lighter tone.

Her insides jumped, and his eyes narrowed. He'd seen her flinch. "I have no idea why I said that." There was a tremor in her voice. "I was just nervous."

"Shall I call you Marr-Car?" he asked.

She huffed and pulled herself from his side, sprinting the rest of the way up the hill. "Absolutely not," she called back. His footsteps drew close. Sensing his nearness, she spun round and held up a hand. "Please don't flirt with me, Mr. Royer," she commanded sternly. "Uncle Liam warned me not to encourage you. Someone back at boarding school apparently said some mean things to ruin my reputation. I wasn't even fully aware of it until Uncle Liam told me. Now, apparently, I have to repair my character, and there can't be the slightest hint of mischief between us. Understood?"

"Understood," he responded in a rough voice as he took a slow step forward, lightly brushing his chest against her small, outstretched hand. The solid, sweaty heat from his body pulsed up her arm and through her pounding heart.

"Good," said Marrin, grabbing the horse's reins from George. Their hands briefly touched before she turned away, urging Pinto to follow, the sense of his hand still tingling in hers.

She spoke a few soft, shaky words to the horse before giving him a "Whoa," so she could fish in the saddlebag for some pins. Working deftly, she folded the soiled portion of her full skirt inward and fixed the fabric in such a way as to hide the sullied area. Satisfied, she stuck a boot into the stirrup and hauled herself back up into the saddle. With a click of her tongue, she turned the horse toward town, still blinking in a fogged blur of emotions. How and why was George always making her feel dizzy, weak, and confused?

"No mischief at all between us?" George asked as he swung onto his own horse and trotted to her side.

"None," she shot back, flashing a cautionary gleam at him before tapping her heels into Pinto's ribs, urging him to pick up the pace. Her calves and thighs ached as she posted in the stirrups and wasn't surprised when George's voice called out in a jumbled blend of English and French, "Keep that up, Sparky, and you'll be tuckered by the time you get to school."

She understood enough and had to admit he was right. When she arrived at the rise of the hill, she pulled too hard on the reins and landed with a teeth-cracking jolt onto the hard saddle. "How far to the schoolhouse?" she asked, peering over the town of Yreka, knowing how challenging it would be to sit on her aching derriere throughout the day.

"Only a few miles now," he said. "Don't worry. You'll be there in plenty of time before school begins." They rode on in silence for a spell. A puff of steam rose in the distance like a misty cloud above the train station, and a whistle blew. As they continued their ride down the other side of the hill, George spoke up again. "You know how I said you were mysterious?" he asked.

"Hm," she nodded, trying to maintain an emotional distance from him.

"I think you're hiding something."

Marrin's stomach muscles seized with tension. "Aren't we all?" she asked, hoping she sounded nonchalant.

"Nope." She could have confronted him about the secret of his mysteriously close relationship with Liam right then, but didn't feel the timing was right.

"I don't necessarily want or need to know all your

secrets," George pushed on, "but I am curious about a few things."

"Like what?" she asked, immediately wishing she could swallow the words.

"Like the fact you really don't seem to be the troublemaking type, yet you're sent all the way out here to live with your uncle as punishment. And you look and dress like a refined, educated young lady, yet some of your mannerisms indicate otherwise."

Her brain tightened within her skull, building pressure behind her eyes. "Do you think I'm lying?" she asked, her voice sounding too defensive.

"I'm curious," he answered with a shrug. "Liam is, too."

"Well, as a matter of fact, I *am* lying, George, about a lot of things. And the truth is the lies are chewing and wrecking my gut." She shouldn't have said it, but she'd been unable to stop herself—as though a dam within her was slowly crumbling and breaking.

"That's because you're a terrible liar," he said. The look on his face was grave.

It might be best to feed him tiny morsels of truth, a little at a time—both to ease her conscience and to keep him and Mr. Stinson from asking so many questions. "I agree. I *am* a terrible liar, George. Holding secrets is so difficult; sometimes I think I'll burst."

The trail widened, and George rode beside her now. "Anything you want to share with me?" he questioned.

She shook her head. "Someday I'm sure I will, yes, but I don't know when or how." She drew a deep breath that nearly brought her shoulders to her ears. "Uncle Liam will be the first to know," she said.

"Wise choice."

"But then he might never want to see me again."

A small lump appeared between George's brows. "Is it something you've done or something that was done to you?"

"I haven't killed anyone, if that's what you're wondering," she said with some irritation.

Their trail finally connected to the road now that they were on the edge of town. They crossed a bridge over a creek that danced and tumbled so noisily over the rocks that it challenged their conversation for a few moments.

"Good to know you're not a murderer," said George when the creek was behind them.

"What I've done will hurt Uncle Liam's heart, I think," she said at last, "but I don't think what's been done really matters to anyone." Why was she saying this to George? Could she trust him with her deepest secrets? Of course, not. And yet something—that breaking dam inside her—felt so good, and she longed to release more of the awful tension.

"Liam could never hate you or anyone else, Carina," said George, a soft, gentle timbre in his voice. "He's eternally kind and forgiving."

"Which is why I hate hurting him," she said, sorrow swelling in her throat.

"And me?"

"Stay away from me, George," she said sternly. "It's for the best."

They were quiet for a time, their horses plodding westward, plowing through a broad, flowery meadow toward a shiny red schoolhouse at the edge of a dense forest of tall pines.

"I lost someone," Marrin finally blurted out. "Someone close to me." It was a piece of truth she thought she could dare to share. "I miss her, and I miss my home in Ami— Belgium." She blinked back the tears gathering at her lashes and berated herself for nearly saying that her home was Amiens. Lying was tricky business.

"I'm sorry, Carina," said George, riding up close and grabbing Pinto's reins to slow the two horses. The small, knotty bump reappeared between his brows. "I don't understand why you can't tell Liam. He'd understand your grief over losing a loved one and being homesick." George shook his head. "I, too, know what it's like to lose someone you love."

She nodded. "Of course, you do. I'm sorry for you, too. The loss of your parents."

"Liam's a good one for listening," he said. "I think you should try talking to him."

"Someday. Maybe."

They rode onward again. Arriving at the school, Marrin slid from her horse before bending to stretch her legs and rub a hand on her aching back. A few small children ran across the meadow toward the school, laughing and shouting to one another. The joy in their voices lifted Marrin's spirits from the darkness she'd slogged through in her heavy conversation with George.

She grinned broadly. "On a glorious morning like this, my first day of school at this charming little schoolhouse, I want to forget everything bad in my life and believe that only good things can happen to me from now on."

"That's the spirit!"

She and George tied their horses to the hitching post in the schoolyard as more children arrived and began kicking a leather ball around a level patch of dust. Laughter and conversation mingled with birdsong as Marrin made her way up the schoolhouse steps. George followed close behind at a quick jog to open the door for her. He stepped close behind her, close enough that she felt the warmth of him without being touched. "Please don't touch me," she croaked in a hoarse whisper.

A befuddled look flashed across his face. "I beg your pardon, mademoiselle," he said, withdrawing his hand. "Miss Trimble will …be here…shortly," he said haltingly.

The small classroom was neat and clean with several tidy rows of desks and chairs. A chalkboard at the front of the room had the remains of a former mathematics lesson, as well as a list of vocabulary words that seemed to be related to geography, if she wasn't mistaken.

"Do you want me to stay and introduce you?" George asked.

"Would you?" she asked, her nerves tense.

"Of course," he said. "I used to sit here." He slapped a desktop and opened a creaky wooden lid. "Noisy as ever," he chuckled. "I should bring some oil for this."

Marrin turned in a slow circle, taking in the details of the room, marveling at the two back walls at the entrance that were lined floor to ceiling with books. A ladder was propped against the shelves.

When the teacher arrived, George introduced her to the prim and petite Miss Trimble, and Marrin's trepidation increased. George explained that "Carina" was new in town from Belgium and didn't speak English, but the schoolmarm gave her only the slightest twitch of a lip. Not a friendly greeting.

"Have a good day, Carina," said George. "I'll be back to escort you home after school." His parting words left Marrin with a strange sense of foreboding.

Miss Trimble pointed to a desk in the front row and sighed audibly as she rattled off something she couldn't understand. Tapping a desk that was apparently meant for her, the teacher yanked open the wooden top and removed some of its contents before stomping to the second row, where she dumped the items into the belly of another desk. Slamming the lid, Miss Trimble dust-clapped her hands, shook her head, and tsk'd before returning to the front of the room, where she wrote with a smooth, beautiful script on the blackboard. The words were foreign to Marrin, and she stood silent and not comprehending as she watched the teacher stomp down the aisle to the front porch, where she rang the bell for students to begin class.

Marrin took her assigned seat at the desk that she assumed was hers; then twisted in her seat to watch wide-eyed as children of all ages entered, casting furtive glances in her direction, and whispering. Heat burned her cheeks. She recognized some of the girls from church on Sunday, but she hated being the center of attention—especially when it felt negative.

When Marrin saw that every student stood beside his or her desk like soldiers at attention, their eyes riveted upon the United States flag displayed at the front of the classroom, she stood and did likewise. When the class recited the "Pledge of Allegiance," she pretended to know the words, although she was unprepared for the unified shout of "One country, one language, one flag!"

Miss Trimble said something, and all students took their seats. Marrin did the same. *One language,* Marrin thought. She'd better learn English faster. Speaking a foreign language was clearly not tolerated. She glanced around, copying other students as they folded their hands on the tops of their desks and kept their eyes riveted upon the teacher. Marrin waited with nervous patience for whatever might come next.

"Psst!"

The teacher was facing the blackboard, scribbling as she spoke.

"Psst!"

Marrin glanced sideways to see a girl waving her sunbonnet at Marrin.

"Oh!" She untied the strings and dragged the bonnet from her head, crumpling and nervously twisting it in her lap.

"Miss Carina Lejeune joins us from Belgium in Europe," Miss Trimble said, turning back to the class. She said more that Marrin couldn't understand, but she did recognize words of greeting from the other students. She nodded and smiled politely at a few faces near her.

"Carina, would you mind sharing a little about your home country before we begin our work for the day?" Miss Trimble stepped aside and gestured, prompting her to speak.

"Stand, please."

Carina stood but froze. Over two dozen faces stared at her, waiting. Her English was so broken, and she knew very little about Belgium.

"Carina?" Miss Trimble tapped a ruler against her palm, and her voice was sharp.

"Je suis désolé. I am sorry. I do not speak good…um…Anglais." It was the truth, and it was her only escape.

Miss Trimble huffed loudly and slapped the ruler hard against her palm. "We speak only English in this classroom, this town, this state, and this country." She ordered her new student to sit.

Marrin was humiliated, yet able to breathe a little more easily. Suddenly, the rest of the class knew what to do and went about doing it. She tried to mimic them. A little girl at the desk beside her waved her slate and a piece of chalk.

Marrin lifted her desk lid with a squeak that made all the other students shoot an eye to her and then to the teacher. She slowly, carefully pulled out chalk and a slate; then closed the lid with another noisy creak.

She rotated the piece of chalk in her fingers. What was she supposed to write? She looked to a neighbor girl for help and decided to copy her work:

$1 + 1 = 2, 1 + 2 = 3$

Too simple. Mercifully, she knew more arithmetic than this. She looked at an older student's work and copied what was written on his slate:

$36 \times 20 = 720$

Yes, she could do this. She continued with problems for an hour, scribbling, working the math, erasing, and starting over with new problems. At one point, Miss Trimble walked slowly past, checking her work. Since she made no comment, Marrin assumed she was on the right track. So far, so good.

And then… Miss Trimble spewed a stream of rapid

sentences directed at another girl in the classroom—a young lady who looked to be about her own age. Marrin's heart jerked with sympathy for the poor girl. Marrin was unaware that her jaw had dropped open until her piece of chalk fell to the floor and rolled under her chair. She clamped her teeth and slipped from her seat to retrieve the stub just as Miss Trimble slammed a ruler onto the other girl's knuckles.

Without thinking, Marrin jumped up, hitting her head on the side of her desk as she rose. Leaping to the teacher, she tore the ruler from Miss Trimble's hand and shook it in her face.

"How dare you hurt an innocent young woman?!" Marrin heard herself speak the words in French before she realized what she was doing. She felt the wide eyes of twenty students burn into her. Miss Trimble's face was tight with fury. Marrin let the ruler clatter to the floor as she meekly apologized for disrupting the class.

Miss Trimble's voice shook as she spoke in a low tone, "One country, one language, one flag." Then something about "English only" and other words, Marrin couldn't understand. The teacher gestured to the skirt of her dress, which had come unpinned in one section, revealing a streak of caked mud. Next, she pointed to a stool in the front corner of the classroom. Was she to sit on the chair? Would she have to wear a dunce cap, too? Miss Trimble pointed again, and Marrin walked forward hesitantly, looking questioningly at the other students. A boy nodded with a worried expression. Setting herself primly on the stool, she maintained an erect posture and held her head high as she faced the corner. Miss Trimble could ridicule and punish her, but she refused to be ashamed for defending an innocent student. No matter what the girl had done or said, it did not warrant a beating. She re-pinned her skirt to hide the mud. She couldn't care less about the soiled fabric. She did care that her first day of school might be her last.

Except for the loud ticking of a clock, the classroom

was silent as students went on working. She even heard a quiet whimpering for a short while—possibly from the girl who'd been disciplined with the ruler. From time to time, Miss Trimble's footsteps could be heard moving about the room. Occasionally, there was a pause as she instructed a student in a voice barely above a whisper.

Marrin took deep breaths and shifted on the hard stool. Her legs ached from dangling inches above the smoothly sanded wood floor. Slowly, carefully, she ventured a peek over her shoulder to catch Miss Trimble's back to her. A few eyes peered back, and she ignored the stares, sure that everyone judged her for being a disobedient immigrant.

The clock on the back wall read half past nine. How long would she be forced to sit on this stool? On the positive side, she hadn't been expelled. Yet. Maybe she hadn't ruined her chances at the education she wanted. But there had to be an easier way. If she were kicked out, was there another school she could attend? Or could she possibly study on her own using Uncle Liam's books?

Her derriere was already sore from riding horseback; now it ached from the hard wooden stool. She wiggled to sit on her hands. When a hint of regret niggled at her conscience, she reminded herself of the beaten girl's knuckles. No, she would not be sorry for defending her fellow student, although she did regret her lack of self-control. She should have remained calmer in addressing Miss Trimble's disciplinary measures. She should have thought first before speaking instead of reacting emotionally. If Miss Trimble demanded an apology, that's exactly what she'd say if she could think of how to say it in English.

At ten o'clock, Miss Trimble summoned her to follow her outside and onto the front porch. When the door shut behind them, Marrin encountered a sharp finger shaking in her face as the teacher scolded her. She was glad she couldn't understand all the words. Marrin's attempt at an apology in a blend of English and French only further exasperated the schoolmarm, who shouted, "English only!"

That's it, thought Marrin. *This is my first and final day of school. I didn't come here to be mistreated and yelled at. I had enough of that back home in France, and I would have had it as an indentured servant in Virginia.* She decided she hated school and wanted out. She seriously considered marching down the steps and mounting her horse right then and there, but she'd left her lunch pail on a shelf in the classroom. She could walk back in to retrieve it and leave, but…

Liam's eyes flickered in her mind. He had been kind enough to provide a place for her to live, food to eat, clothes to wear—and this opportunity to receive an education. Even though she wasn't Carina, she wanted to make Mr. Stinson proud. Perhaps she could give Miss Trimble another chance and try to endure two more hours. Liam would probably send her right back to school anyhow.

She nodded to the teacher and did her best to apologize in her broken English and was invited to return to the classroom.

English just happened to be her next course of study, and she pleasantly surprised herself with how much she was able to comprehend in the McGuffey's Eclectic Primer she was given. It was meant for young readers, but she didn't mind. It served to build her confidence. She skipped around in the book and happened upon the lines:

Do you see that tall tree? Long ago,
it sprang up from a small nut.

Do you know who made it
so? It was God, my child.

God made the world and all
things in it.

God? Her eyes were drawn to the window. She'd never known what to think of God. She believed in Him, but He'd allowed her parents to die, done nothing to help when she'd been forced to live with horrible relatives, and done nothing to save her from slavery. She'd had to rescue herself. God might have created the world and all things in it, and she wanted to attend church to make new friends, but she didn't feel like worshiping Him.

Lunchtime presented a new worry to Marrin. Assuming no one would want a foreigner for a friend, she asked Miss Trimble if she could remain at her desk to eat and maybe continue with her reading. The answer was a firm no. She had to join the other students outdoors to get some fresh air before it might start to rain.

With drooping head and shoulders, Marrin stepped outside and was immediately attacked by a huddle of several pawing, chattering girls. And the girl who'd received the ruler beating squeezed her in a long, tight hug! Tripping and nearly tumbling, Marrin was practically carried down the porch steps by the girls. And it was then that she heard a most beautiful sound. Words in French!

"You were wonderful," a girl said in a mess of French and English. Marrin shook her head. She certainly wasn't wonderful. "Nobody likes the beatings with the ruler. It is wrong, and you told Miss Trimble so. Nobody has dared this before. And don't worry. I will teach you English." Marrin shook her head again, dazed and unsure if she was fully comprehending.

"We will all teach you English," said another girl.

The girls introduced themselves. Collette Marchand was the one who could speak some French, because her parents and grandparents spoke the language. Milly was the hugger. She couldn't quite catch or remember the names of the other girls, but she'd learn in time. The important thing was that she'd not only learn English, but she had unexpectedly made new friends on her very first day! She could barely remember the last time she'd had a friend. Besides George, if he even counted. She'd had many friends in elementary school years ago…before her parents died.

Suddenly, she didn't care how many scoldings she received from Miss Trimble. School wasn't going to be so bad, after all.

CHAPTER 11:
Puppy Love

"When you fish for love, bait with your heart, not your brain." –Mark Twain

Outside the schoolhouse at the close of the day, Marrin tied on her sunbonnet and was startled at the absurd way Collette, Milly, and the other girls giggled and talked too loudly about the dashing gentleman approaching on horseback. Marrin rolled her eyes and shook her head at George, doing her best to act normal. Yes, he was handsome, but was he worth all the fuss?

She buckled her lunch pail to the saddlebag and hauled herself onto Pinto's back before grabbing the reins and turning east toward home just as sprinkles of rain began to fall. "Want me to introduce you to them?" she asked George, giving her new friends a parting wave. His cheeks turned red. "You're not blushing, are you, George?" she teased.

He rubbed the back of his neck. "Embarrassed is all."

"Hm. Haven't you courted much?" she asked as they rode side by side down the rain-spattered road. The color in his cheeks deepened, and there was no reply. "Well, I'm surprised."

"You thought this handsome gentleman had gone

courting with lots of young ladies?"

"I thought someone who flirts as audaciously as you must have had substantial practice with the ladies," she said, her tone snide.

George cleared his throat. "I guess I flirted some in school, but…"

"But not much *real* courting?" she interrupted. He shook his head. "Why not?"

He shrugged. "I never wanted to court a girl just for fun. Guess I want to wait to find a girl I want to marry. Am I too old-fashioned?"

She lifted and dropped her shoulders. "I didn't think you were the serious type."

"I am, actually, and I apologize for appearing too casual with you, mademoiselle." Marrin choked on a lump in her throat. Was he feeling serious about her? "I shouldn't casually tease a girl and make her think I like her too much."

"No, you should not," Marrin admonished, angry that his words stung like needles in her chest. "You mean you don't want me to think you like me too much."

"No, that's not…what I'm saying," George stammered. "I do like you." His hoarse voice melted the needles into a pool of wax. She didn't know what to say, but she had to say something to keep him from liking her too much because of Liam's warning.

"I…like you too," she said hesitantly, "but as a friend. I can't let Uncle Liam think of me as some sort of trollop, you know."

"Oh, a friend." She was unable to see his face, but his tone was flat. For a long moment, only the sound of hooves hitting the earth filled the silence. Then he cleared his throat. "How was school for you today?" he asked.

Grateful for the safer topic, she launched into a tale of Miss Trimble, the altercation, and sitting on the stool in the corner. He listened without interrupting, letting her fill the space between them with words that kept her from thinking too hard about what they'd said to one another earlier.

It was raining harder as they dismounted and untacked their horses in the shelter of the barn. Pain screamed in every muscle of her body, and she moved slowly, stretching her back as she removed the rain-soaked sunbonnet from her head and stuffed it into her empty lunch pail.

"You'll need another hot bath and some liniment," said George.

Lighting flashed, followed by rumbles of thunder as Jacques, the sheepdog, bounded into the barn and burrowed into a haystack in a corner. George and Marrin laughed at the poor pup, and George took a moment to step over and reassure him that the storm was harmless. Marrin kept her distance.

"Look at Carina," George said to Jacques. "I'm not sure she likes you too much."

"I like dogs a little," Marrin argued.

George stood and brushed a few blades of hay from his trousers. "Bad experience with a dog in the past, Sparky?"

Marrin avoided George's gaze and fumbled with the safety pin on her skirt. "I did, actually."

"What kind of dog?" George asked, sympathy reflected in his countenance.

"Just a dog." Marrin removed the safety pin from her skirt and tucked it into a pocket.

George stepped closer. "A big, mean dog?"

"I don't want to talk about it."

He drew nearer. "How big and mean was this dog?"

"You'll laugh."

"I'm laughing a little bit already."

Marrin stood arms akimbo and glared. "It was a very mean Dachshund."

George's eyes expanded. "You mean one of those tiny--?"

"Tiny but mean!" Marrin nearly shouted. "He clamped onto my calf and would not let go! I shook and shook, but someone had to pull him off. It was frightful!"

George guffawed outright, and Marrin pouted. "I never promised not to laugh," he said.

"Thank you for your sympathy, Mr. Royer, and for taking time out of your day to escort me to school and back. Bon soir." She turned and walked toward the open barn door, ready to make a dash through a downpour to the house. He caught her elbow—firm, sudden. Spinning her toward him, the barn wall met her back. Her breath caught, and her vision fluttered. His face was so close, and the warmth of his touch on her arm seared like hot embers. All stiffness in her limbs dissolved and threatened to turn her to liquid.

Lightning lit the shadows, and his mouth hovered a mere breath from hers. "Mademoiselle, once you convince Liam of your good character, will you consider me more than a friend?" George asked, the sweet aroma of soap, cinnamon, and leather teasing her nostrils.

As he leaned toward her ever so slightly, she longed for his lips to touch hers.

"Well?" he asked.

"Well?" she repeated hoarsely.

"Someday, could you possibly think of me with death, rather than friendship?" he asked in French.

She giggled despite herself. "Death?"

"What did I say?" He wrinkled his brows. "Did I mix up my words again?"

She nodded, unable to suppress her smile. "La mort is death. L'amour is love," she said, relieved that his spell on her had broken.

"L'amour," George repeated slowly, as if committing it to memory. "Carina, I'm serious. Do you think you could ever think of me with love and not mere friendship?" His chest so close to hers, along with his pleading hazel-gray eyes searching her face, made it hard to find her next breath.

"Maybe," she whispered. It was the truth. For now. Per

both Liam's warning and her situation in which she would someday have to run away from this place, she couldn't love this man long-term, but in this moment, he was tempting her beyond reason. She wanted to forget about Liam. She wanted George to hold her, to absorb her body into his. She lifted her chin slightly and almost moved her mouth a centimeter closer to his when a loud crack of thunder saved her from the brink of a terrible mistake.

"George, I…I," she panted haltingly. "I don't think of you as more than a friend. Not yet."

"No, of course, not," he whispered.

"Besides, there are things you don't know about me," she said, trying to sound stern.

"More secrets?" he asked.

She nodded. "And there's Uncle Liam."

"I don't care about your secrets. Well, maybe I should, but I can't. And I'll ask Liam if I can court you. Maybe I can change his mind," he said, already sounding unsure of it.

But Marrin knew Liam would *not* understand. She wriggled away from George and stood in the barn doorway, looking out at the rain. She had such mixed feelings. She wanted George but didn't want to lead him on when she'd eventually have to leave. She couldn't hurt this man. And she was lying to him about everything. She wasn't who he thought she was, and she'd never be able to tell him the truth.

"No, George. Now is not the time. You're a hired ranch hand, and I'm Liam's niece. He'd oppose our courtship for that reason, as well as the fact that he has forbidden me from consorting with you. And I must work to repair my reputation."

"Do you feel anything for me at all?" His voice enveloped her, squeezing her heart.

She shook her head. "I…I don't think so." She made the mistake of looking back at him and sucked in her breath.

"I…I don't know." His eyes held hers with an intensity that made her resolve crumble like a sandcastle smashed by waves. "I don't know."

"I can talk to him," said George. "He thinks of me as a son."

"Why is that?" she asked.

"It's a long story."

"So, you do have secrets?"

His voice was deep and tender. "And I hope to share them with you someday."

He stood beside her and waited for a break in the rain before dashing with her across the barnyard to the house. They stamped up the porch steps, where they seated themselves in separate chairs to remove their muddy boots.

Tiptoeing in stockings, George opened the door for her to enter the house ahead of him, pressing a quick whisper to her ear that sent warm shivers through her body. "I'm going to talk to Liam about us," he said.

"No, not yet," she returned. "I'm not sure…"

"Carina!" Liam's voice called from the parlor. "Come in. I have a surprise for you."

"After you," said George, tipping his hat and gesturing to Marrin with a hand that held her lunch pail and bonnet as he closed the door behind them. She grabbed the pail and set it on a bench inside the foyer before sweeping ahead of George to the parlor.

Marrin froze with surprise when both Mr. Stinson and another man rose to greet her.

"Look who showed up to surprise us," beamed Liam.

"Bonjour, Carina," said the gentleman.

Marrin forced her face to register what she hoped was surprise, rather than confusion. "Oh, my!" she said. "I…I can't believe it's you." Who was he? He was rather good-looking and well-dressed, but why did he address her so informally, and…

"Not exactly the reaction I expected, Carina," the man

said, leaning in to kiss her cheek. She jerked backward and swung her hand upward to slap him in the face, stopping just in time to give in to the kissing formality. Was this man related to Carina?

"What's wrong, Carina?" the gentleman asked. "You act as though you've never seen me before."

Her mind stopped, faltered. "It's just been such a long time," she said shakily. Who was he? And why was he displaying such familiar boldness toward her—in front of Uncle Liam? And in front of George? Her ears throbbed with panic, and the room suddenly felt tight and cramped. Was the real Carina here, too? Carina wouldn't do that to her, would she?

"Please, sit with us, both of you," Liam invited, gesturing to a settee.

Marrin seated herself beside George, forcing a smile to the strange man as she continued to wonder about him. "You've gone and grown up, Carina," said the man. "You were just a snip of a girl when I saw you last. I hardly recognize you."

Her heart slightly slowed its pounding. His not recognizing her was some consolation. But she wished Uncle Liam would introduce the man to George, so she'd know who he was.

"Who is he?" George whispered in her ear when the strange man wasn't looking.

If only she knew! He and Carina were obviously well-acquainted. The only times men kissed women on the cheeks was if they were cousins or… Or brother and sister. Was this Carina's *brother*? Her heart rate somersaulted again. If he was, she'd have to avoid him like the plague, or he'd catch her in a mess of lies. What was his name again? Aaron? No. Alan? Albert? Alden?

Alard!

CHAPTER 12:
Snake in the House

"Never allow someone to be your priority while allowing yourself to be their option." — Generally attributed to Mark Twain

"*A*re you feeling better this morning?" Edith asked when Marrin tried to skirt past the sitting room and hide in the kitchen to eat something before school. "You skipped dinner last night."

"I'm feeling better," she lied. "Thank you, Edith." She'd managed to steer clear of Liam, George, and Alard the previous evening by feigning a headache. But she hadn't really been pretending. Alard's presence made her feel sick all over.

"Mr. Stinson wants you to breakfast with him in the parlor."

"Yes, ma'am," said Marrin, bobbing in a curtsy. "Oh, sorry." She shook her head. "I keep forgetting."

"You've got quite a habit of the curtsys," Edith snorted.

"I know. I'm trying to stop."

Edith gave Marrin a small tsk as though she knew something about her questionable past. *Carina's* past, not hers. "You'd better get on in there," Edith prompted, tilting her head to the parlor door before picking up a tray of sweet corn pudding topped with melted butter and hot maple syrup. "After you, dear."

Marrin inhaled slowly, attempting in vain to steady her breath before proceeding to the parlor. She seated herself at a small round table by a window. George entered and slid onto a chair beside her as Edith placed the bowls of corn pudding before them.

"Say a prayer and eat up," Edith ordered. "Mr. Stinson won't mind that you've started without him. He knows you have school, Carina."

Marrin bowed her head. *God, how can Carina's brother be here? And thank you for this food. Amen.*

"Ton cheval est joli," said George after their moment of silence.

"My horse is pretty?" Marrin asked.

"Oh, no," he groaned. "I mixed up my words again." She allowed her lips to curve a touch. He switched to English. "I meant to say your hair is pretty."

She blushed and patted her head. "Thank you. Just…please don't say such a thing when Uncle Liam is here."

"So, your brother, Alard," he said, changing the subject. Marrin scowled and said nothing, opting to keep her mouth full. He leaned across the table to her. "You really don't like your brother, do you?"

"Not at all," she whispered.

"You'll have to tell me more on the way to school." She shrugged and scooped another bite into her mouth, staring into her bowl. The silence stretched. Maybe if she kept chewing, he'd stop asking questions. George reached out and touched her hand. "Slow down," he said. "You're eating like a ranch hand again."

She tightened her jaw and nearly threw her spoon into the bowl. "I can't seem to do anything right," she muttered.

"What's that?" asked George.

"Nothing." She settled the spoon and raised a cup of

hot coffee to her lips; then stopped. Her hand shook so uncontrollably that she nearly spilled the drink. Managing a sip, she wondered if Alard would notice her lack of manners. Of course, he would. She wouldn't eat anything if he came into the room.

"Are you all right, Carina?" asked George as Liam and Alard entered the parlor. "You're shaking."

"I'm fine," she said in a low voice, placing her spoon on the breakfast tray. Carina's uncle and brother seated themselves at the shared round table. "I apologize, Uncle Liam, for starting our breakfast without you," Marrin said.

"I don't mind at all," he returned. "You don't want Miss Trimble to put you in the corner." Marrin nearly choked as Liam's eyes crinkled at the corners. She shot a piercing eye at George, and he shook his head, his eyes wide.

"How's school, Carina?" Alard asked jovially, shoveling a mouthful of corn pudding into his cheeks and disregarding Uncle Liam's moment of prayer.

Marrin waited until Liam raised his head. "I've attended only one day of school so far, and it's pleasant enough, merci, Alard." She touched her napkin to her lips and laid it neatly on the table beside her near-empty bowl. "And now, if you'll excuse me, I really must leave for school. It's nice to see you again, brother." She nodded to Mr. Stinson. "Uncle Liam."

Alard snorted. "Well, aren't you all prim and proper, Carina?"

Marrin felt the muscles in her jaw harden like knotted ropes. "I try," she said, her words pinched and tight.

"I can see that," said Alard, planting his elbows on the table and ramming another spoonful of mush into his mouth.

Who was eating like a ranch hand now? She pushed back her chair and stood. Liam and George were probably now wondering if her lack of manners stemmed from Carina and Alard's parents. It might make them more sympathetic to her many faux pas. She rose, and both George and Liam stood politely. Alard did not.

Marrin slid her chair back beneath the table and addressed George, "Take your time finishing breakfast. I'll be ready in a few minutes." He nodded.

"You two are on such familiar terms?" asked Alard. Both George and Marrin ignored him. "What are you, George? A ranch hand? A chauffeur?"

"George manages my entire ranch, and he's like a son to me, so I'll ask you to treat him with respect," Liam said curtly.

"Yes, sir," Alard said, speaking with his mouth full and shrugging. "Did you have Madame Renard back at Sint-Katelijne-Waver School, Carina?" Alard spluttered, oblivious to a chunk of corn that shot from his mouth onto the tablecloth. "I knew some girls from Sint-Katelijne-Waver who talked about her."

Marrin froze before forcing a nonchalant expression onto her face. "Oh, Madame Renard," she said, waving a hand in the air. "Oui, I heard stories about her, but never had her for a teacher. Excuse me again. I really must hurry." She lifted her skirt and hurried up the stairs to her room as fast as her aching legs could carry her.

Her whole body shook like the rumbling of a train station platform. This was going to keep happening as long as Alard was here, asking her questions she couldn't truthfully answer, and everyone would expect her to know things about her childhood with him that she didn't know. He'd expect her to talk about memories he and Carina shared as children. This was serious. Every word she spoke risked giving her away.

She brushed her teeth, dropping the toothbrush twice and striking the side of her mouth with the bristles, making a chalky mess of her chin. Splashing water onto her face, Marrin peered at herself in the glass above the wash basin. She wasn't bad-looking. Her light café au lait eyes were bright in skin that was slowly darkening with hours spent in the sun of the past several days. Her molasses curls were pinned in a Gibson style that George had admired. She hoped the locks wouldn't tumble loose before school ended.

She drew a breath and exhaled. George. She had to forget about him. Alard's being here ruined everything. If Alard didn't leave right away, she'd have to make her escape sooner than anticipated. It was just a matter of time before Alard figured out she wasn't Carina.

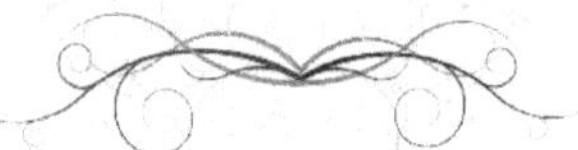

Think, Marrin! she told herself. She needed to send an emergency telegram to Carina.

Seated on Pinto, she rode out of the barnyard with George trotting ahead of her. Reaching into an empty skirt pocket, she felt for any coins she might have with her, but the pocket was empty, save for a handkerchief. Should she run back to her room? No, she was running late. She'd have to stop by the telegraph office tomorrow. What should she write?

"So?" George tossed back over his shoulder.

"Pardon me?" she asked, impatient with his interruption of her thoughts.

"Tell me about Alard," said George. "When was the last time you saw him?"

She faltered. "Um, years ago, but I heard a rumor he got into some trouble with the law once."

The trail widened, and George rode alongside her. A smile edged up one of his cheeks. "Well, that rumor can't be true. He doesn't look or act like an outlaw. His manners are a little rough, but he doesn't strike me as a criminal."

Marrin wished George would keep quiet and let her think for a few minutes. "Looks are deceiving." *Truer than you realize*, she thought.

"Aren't you overreacting a little?"

"He was never kind to me, George, and I don't want to talk about him." The words were spoken with finality, in hopes of ending the discussion.

It worked. George remained quiet for the remainder of their trip to the schoolhouse, where Marrin was greeted by her new friends. She thanked George and gave him a quick wave goodbye. He must think her very rude, but she couldn't find the presence of mind to be courteous and conversational. Alard could never discover that she was not Carina. She needed a plan. Fast.

Aside from tripping over her own feet mounting the schoolhouse steps that morning, the day passed with relatively few mishaps for Marrin. She was scolded for nervously bouncing her knee and tapping a finger on her desktop but overall, she behaved herself and did well in her lessons. During lunch recess, Collette helped her practice a few English phrases, and she enjoyed getting to know Milly and the other girls—although they talked incessantly about George and other boys in town.

Friends. She was finally in a place where loneliness was beginning to fade. How she'd hate to leave!

While the girls giggled about love and courtship, Marrin continued to fret about Alard. Tomorrow, she'd leave school early to send a telegram before George arrived to escort her back to the ranch. Then there was the problem of a reply from Carina. If Carina sent a telegram back to Marrin, she could expect a wire from her right away. But the letter she'd written wouldn't reach Belgium until mid-July at the earliest. By then, who knew what could happen? She'd have to send both—the telegram with very few details and the letter with a full explanation.

On the way home after school, she asked George if he thought she was ready to ride to and from school alone. The alarm that registered on his face declared a definite no. He also told her it was useless to ask Liam about it. She'd expected as much, but it hadn't hurt to ask.

As they approached the arched gate of Greenwind Ranch, Marrin asked George what the circle with the "M" inside meant.

"It's Liam's ranch brand," he explained. "He uses it to brand all his cattle, so everyone knows which cattle are his."

"But what does it mean?"

"It's a little mystery," George said. "Ask him sometime."

Riding into the farmyard, Marrin's nerves grew taut and stretched with dread at facing Alard again. Immediately, Pinto began to act up, tossing his head, walking sideways, refusing to move forward.

"What's wrong with him?" Marrin asked, tightening her grip on the saddle horn.

"He's nervous about something," said George. "It might be from your nervousness, Carina. You need to remain calm and speak softly to settle him." She tried to do as George instructed, but it was impossible. In seconds, George was off his horse and gripping Pinto's bridle while he stroked the horse's broad cheek. "Hand me the reins," he commanded roughly. She obeyed and held on more tightly to keep from falling. "What's wrong, Carina? You're shaking like an earthquake."

"It's this horse," she said breathlessly.

George shook his head. "I don't think so. I think you spooked him."

"I did not," she bit back.

"Never mind. I want you to try to dismount, and I'll catch you."

"No, I can't let go," Marrin insisted.

"Do as I say, Carina," he said so sternly; she was startled into compliance. He caught her just as Pinto decided to rear. George dropped the reins and held her tightly in his arms, cradling her like a child and nearly dropping her as he stumbled backward.

"What's going on out here?" a man's voice asked amidst a cloud of dust.

"Not much," said George, setting Marrin's feet back on solid ground.

"Looked like you were rescuing Carina from a bucking horse." It was Alard and his words that sent a cold shiver down Marrin's spine.

"Nope," said George, "nothing that dramatic. Your sister's just a little clumsy, is all. She's fine now."

Marrin pushed herself from George's embrace and dusted off her skirt. "Good afternoon, Alard," she said, her hands and voice trembling.

"Good afternoon?" he asked. "So formal, Carina. And since when have you ever been clumsy? You've always been steady on your feet."

"I guess you don't remember me, Alard," Marrin shot back, steel in her tone.

"I remember you were always good with horses," Alard argued.

"Then your memory is dimmer than I thought," she retorted. "I never rode well, and I've never been very coordinated. If you remember otherwise, your memory is bad."

"Or you deceive me," Alard said, his deep voice dark, almost menacing.

Marrin's face went hot with confusion. "I…I led Maman et Papa to believe I loved horses and rode well, because I wanted them to love me. Even you know that." Angry that a drop of moisture escaped her eyes, she stomped to the house, not caring that both men stared after her.

Alard jogged over to her and took her elbow, but she jerked it away. "I'm sorry if I made you cry, Carina," he said.

"I'm not crying, and I don't need your sympathy," she

shot back defensively.

He stopped and whistled. "I forgot what a viper you could be, Rina."

"You forget a lot of things," she said, spinning on her heel and shaking a finger at him. "And don't call me that, Alard."

He laughed heartily. "You never did like being called Rina."

She turned away and banged up the porch steps and into the house, slamming the door behind her, wondering what she was doing, saying things so impulsively. She had to be more careful, or she'd say something truly incriminating.

CHAPTER 13:
Borrowed Time

"The fear of death follows from the fear of life. A man who lives fully is prepared to die at any time." –Mark Twain

*H*eart pounding, she leaned against the wall in the foyer and looked back through the sheer curtains to the driveway where Alard and George stood looking toward the house.

"I forgot how much she and I hate each other," she heard Alard say.

George nodded and walked away in one direction, Alard in another. As she sat on a bench to remove her boots, she regretted leaving George to tend to both horses, but she was too emotionally and physically exhausted, as well as muscle-sore, to go back out to help. She'd apologize later. First, she needed to get up to her room, where she could avoid Alard and think through some way to make him leave before she would be forced to do so herself.

On the pretense of fatigue and needing to complete schoolwork, Marrin skipped another dinner with Liam, George, and Alard that evening, telling Edith she wasn't

hungry—which was a lie. She added more to the letter she'd written to Carina, informing her of Alard's sudden appearance at Greenwind Ranch and her fears that he'd discover she was an imposter. She sealed the envelope and wrote "Carina Lejeune" in the return address section of the envelope. Yes, it looked strange that it was also addressed to Carina Lejeune, but who would notice? She slipped the letter between the pages of Mr. Stinson's copy of *Tom Sawyer*, then tightened the belt strap around it and her other schoolbooks.

When she heard the guffaws and low, muffled voices of Liam, George, and Alard rumbling behind the dining room doors as their supper commenced, Marrin slipped out of her bedroom and shimmied down the carpeted hallway to the guest bedroom where Alard was staying. She turned the knob until it clicked open. She pushed herself inside and carefully shut the door behind her.

There was still plenty of light shining through the sheer curtains, which allowed her to peruse the room's contents. She located Alard's suitcase tucked beneath the bed and scurried over to tug it out and plop it onto the bed with a noisy creak of the mattress springs. She stopped, holding her breath, staring at the door—the bellowing of voices carried on downstairs. Fingers quivering, she unlatched the case and carefully lifted out items of clothing onto the bed in search of something hidden beneath. She wanted to find something that implicated him as the criminal Carina had said he was. Something stolen? How would she know it was stolen? An incriminating note? Identification papers that revealed suspicious places he'd traveled?

Wait! Tucked into the sleeve of a white cotton shirt was a stack of crisp, neat bills. She froze. She'd never seen so much money before! She could use some of it to make her escape! She wouldn't need much. Maybe fifty…or maybe one hundred dollars. Maybe a little more. But she wasn't a thief. Well, actually, she had been once. But stealing a linen coat on a ship one time didn't make her a thief. What if she stole a second time? But was it really theft if she robbed a thief?

Before she had time to talk herself out of it, she pocketed two hundred and fifty dollars and gingerly replaced the stack of bills in the shirt sleeve before picking through more of the suitcase. It wasn't until she lifted up a pair of brown- and black-striped trousers that she felt cold steel beneath her fingertips and spied the metallic shine of a revolver. Heart hammering into her throat, she dropped the gun and closed the suitcase lid, snapping it shut before sliding it beneath the bed.

Most men probably carried guns in the west, but to live down the hall from a man with a revolver and a pile of money—a man who'd been described by his own sister as an outlaw? That was terrifying! But now what? Tell Liam? Tell George? To do so meant revealing her sin of trespassing, not to mention her theft if that money was found in her possession. Of course, she could tell no one.

Tiptoeing across the room, Marrin stepped to the door and held her breath, listening. Silence. Nothing. No talking, no laughter, no clink of dishes. Her heart thudded into her stomach, shoving bile upward. Where were the men? Had they finished dinner so soon? Could they have already retired for the evening? *Could Alard be on his way upstairs?*

A knock pounded nearby, and Marrin's heart leaped into her windpipe, locking her breath. She held still, every muscle in her body tense, waiting. The knock sounded again, but it wasn't on Alard's door; it was down the hall. Maybe…

"Carina?" It was Edith's voice calling.

Marrin waited, hoping the housekeeper wouldn't go into her room and find it empty. Footsteps padded on the hallway past Alard's door and down the stairs. Her muscles relaxed, and she crept to the door, leaning against it, listening again. The steps receded, and the house stilled.

Where were the men? Outside? She was anxious to escape the room, but she had more searching to do—even though she doubted she'd find anything more shocking than loads of money and a gun.

She tiptoed to the wardrobe and opened the doors, feeling in every shirt and coat pocket, probing inside Alard's boots. Nothing. She felt around for anything else hidden in the wardrobe. Nothing. Closing the wardrobe doors, she knelt on the floor and opened a drawer beneath the piece of furniture, fingering socks and other articles of clothing. Nothing. If only she knew what she was looking for….

The muffled sound of men's voices rose from the yard below. Marrin slipped to the window and spied George and Liam talking. Not good. Where was Alard? She stole to the door again and halted. All was still quiet, so she turned the knob and pulled the door cautiously inward. No one was about, so she slipped out, closed the door behind her, and scurried down the hall to her bedroom, where a tray of food lay on the floor before the door. She opened the door and picked up the tray.

"Carina?" a man's voice asked.

She spun around with a gasp, nearly spilling the contents of the supper tray on Alard. "Oh!" she cried. "You startled me!"

"A little jumpy, there," he said. "We missed you at supper."

"I wasn't hungry then," she said. "I need to get back to my schoolwork." She turned her back to him and tried to enter her room, but his hand gripped her with a bone-chilling dread on her arm.

"Wait," he said. "I want to talk to you about what you said earlier—about wanting Mother and Father to love you." She paused, listening warily. "I always felt the same way, Rina. Father was neutral toward us, but Mother was a self-centered, conceited woman. She cared more about her parties and friends and public image than her children.

You're lucky she wasn't your real mother."

Marrin felt as though a brick had been slammed into her chest. "What?" she asked, stunned. Even though she wasn't Carina, she still felt the weight of this news.

"You didn't…know?" Alard stuttered.

"Know that Mother isn't my *real* mother?" Marrin's voice squeaked. "What in heaven's name are you talking about?"

"Oh, dear," Alard sighed, rumbling his lips. "If it's any consolation, your real mother wasn't much better than mine."

"What does that mean? And how is that a consolation?" Her voice shook appropriately. She doubted his sincerity. What was his motive for telling her this? And was it even true? "I don't believe you."

"I'm sorry, Rina, I thought you knew."

"I still don't believe you."

"Rina, your real mother was some snobbish socialite who paid my mother to raise her daughter as her own."

"You're lying!" she said, raising her voice.

"No, I'm not. You're what they call *illegitimate*."

"How dare you?!" Marrin cried.

"Calm down, Rina. I'm not lying. I thought you knew. *Everybody* knew. Remember how Mother always found you to be such a nuisance? This is why. And it's why you were sent away to boarding school."

"How dare you?!" Marrin's voice was faint with shock. What did this all mean for her—and Carina? Why did it feel like such a surprise to her when she wasn't even the real Carina?

"She sent me away too," Alard said wryly, "so I don't think she loved either one of us, flesh and blood or not."

Marrin's mind felt crowded, congested, swarming. "Do you think Father—?"

"—had an affair with some woman and took you in, forcing Mother to care for you?" He rolled his eyes.

"Possibly."

"I hadn't thought of that," Marrin muttered. "I can't listen to any of this. I need time alone." She whirled round and abruptly ended their conversation. Entering her room, she shut the door behind her with her foot, set the dinner tray on the desk, and collapsed onto the bed.

A boiling ball churned in her gut as she lay watching golden sunset light flicker leafy shadows on the ceiling. Carina was adopted? Surely Carina didn't know any of this, or she would have told her, right? If Alard was even telling the truth. But why would he lie about this? She'd have to tell Carina. Poor Carina. What a shock this would be to her. She probably wouldn't believe it. She'd have to add all this to her letter or the telegram. The telegram would be easier. But how could she afford such a long note? She had only a few coins....

No! She reached into her skirt pocket and pulled out the bills she'd stolen from Alard's room. She had plenty of money to send a telegram! Plenty of money to make her escape, too.

Suddenly, there was nothing keeping her there. Alard's presence was putting her in danger. She had the means and opportunity to leave, and yet... Yet she was growing fond of Liam and her friends at school and...and George. She didn't know how she could leave. Not now that she finally felt at home.

CHAPTER 14:
A Lost Letter

"You can't depend on your eyes when your imagination is out of focus." — Mark Twain, *A Connecticut Yankee in King Arthur's Court* (1889)

*L*eaving class early the following afternoon, Marrin descended the schoolhouse steps and untied Pinto. Swinging into the saddle, she rode into town, worrying about yesterday's news, Alard's presence, and all that she would write in a telegraphic post to Carina.

As she was about to pass by the sheriff's office, she decided to stop for just a moment. She looped Pinto's reins around the hitching post as George had taught her and climbed the steps to enter the vacant building with its iron-barred brick-lined cell. She shivered. She could end up there.

"Hello?" she called out. No answer. She peered around the dimly lit room. On the walls hung a few old, tattered wanted posters. None featured drawings of a man that looked anything like Alard. The notion that Alard was a criminal must have been mere speculation on Carina's part. And even George had found the idea preposterous. The lack of evidence should have put her mind at ease, but it did not.

She left the sheriff's office and clomped along the

boardwalk to the telegraph office, where she went inside and arranged to send Carina the following message:

ALARD HERE Stop *HELP* Stop *UR ADOPTED* Stop

There. Five words that would shake up Carina's world and make her write back immediately.

"This telegram is going to Belgium?" the telegraph operator asked.

"Yes, ma'am," Marrin replied.

"This is both a very long-distance telegram, ma'am. Do you realize the cost?"

Marrin's heart stopped. "How much?"

"Five words transcontinental and transatlantic," the woman said, shaking her head. "It'll cost you twenty-five dollars."

"Twenty-five dollars?" Marrin's voice was high. "Maybe I do not understand English." She made a motion like she was writing the number 25 in the air.

"Yes," grunted the operator. The woman scribbled out the numbers $25 on a slip of paper and slid it to Marrin.

She gasped. She had the money she'd stolen from Alard, but she didn't want to waste it on this. "Comme c'est terrible." The words slipped out before she could stop them. She had twenty-five dollars with her, but she couldn't spend all of it on a single telegram. She needed money to make her escape and provide for herself.

"Yes, it is terrible," the operator said with a hard crease between her brows. "I'm very sorry. Perhaps you could shorten the message?"

"How much for three words?" she queried.

"Fifteen dollars."

Marrin pressed her fingers to her forehead. "I must think," she muttered as another customer entered.

"I understand," said the woman. "You can have a seat on that bench against the wall if you'd like. Here's a pencil and more paper for you."

Marrin nodded, muttered a thank you, and dropped

heavily onto the bench. What could she write that would cost only a few dollars? She finally settled on a message that still cost the extortionary amount of ten dollars: *ALARD HERE* Stop

Carina would have to hear about being adopted later in her letter.

After the telegraph office, Marrin stopped off at the post office to mail Carina's letter. She stood at the counter and opened the book that held the envelope. It wasn't there! Where could it be? Nerves writhing like worms in her belly, she dashed out of the building and down the street, leaning against Pinto to catch her breath a moment before searching through every other book in the saddlebag. Nothing. No letter. Could she have dropped it? The address along with her name on the front, would arouse loads of suspicion.

Urging Pinto to a gallop, Marrin held tightly, sliding in the saddle as she rounded the bend to the schoolhouse. In her haste, she tumbled to the ground. She picked herself up, dusted off her skirt, and darted up the steps, not slowing until she entered the building. She apologized to Miss Trimble in a whisper as she crept up the aisle to her desk, opened the lid, and searched for the letter. Gone. Where on earth could it be? Surely, if someone in the school had found it, they'd give it back to her, right?

Miss Trimble dismissed the class, and Marrin exited the building along with her classmates just as George was approaching. Their ride home felt strained. They hadn't talked much that morning, and there wasn't much Marrin could think of to say now. She was still embarrassed by her outburst with Alard the previous afternoon.

Marrin felt sick with worry. Was it possible that Alard had seen the letter when he was near her room the day before? Had he stolen it? *Quel cauchemard!* That letter revealed her true identity and how she'd schemed with Carina against Liam Stinson! Her breath came in gasps, her chest tight as if squeezed in a vice. Would Marrin arrive back at Greenwind Ranch to find Mr. Stinson waiting for her with the sheriff? But Liam wouldn't do that without telling George, would he? Her eyes pitched to George and clung to him. He was quiet today. Too quiet.

Pinto suddenly slowed, trotted jerkily, and flared his nostrils, whipping his head up and down.

"Hold on," said George as he rode up. He grabbed Pinto's bridle and spoke gently to him. "You're too tense, Sparky."

"I am not," she said tersely.

"Even I can see you're wound tight as a clock," George bickered. The horse finally halted and snorted out rumbling exhales. "Take a few deep breaths and relax your body and shoulders so Pinto will calm down," George directed.

She did her best to follow his instructions, but fear threatened to send her into a panic as a sob itched in her throat.

"Breathe, Carina," he said softly, tenderly, touching her hand where it grasped the saddle horn. She tried to pull away from George, but his hand was firm, warm, and determined. Comforting. She didn't deserve his kindness. She puffed out a long breath. "There you go," he said, patting and stroking her hand. "What's gotten into you, Sparky? Is it Alard?"

"You know it is," she spat back too sharply. But he had called her Sparky, and the nickname soothed her. Surely, he wouldn't call her that if he'd learned of the contents of her letter.

He removed his hand. "I don't understand. Can you explain? What's between you two?"

She pressed a palm to her eyes and sucked in a damp sniffle. If she didn't say something to someone soon, she'd explode. But, in case Alard hadn't found the letter and hadn't told Liam anything, she didn't dare speak the full truth—to anyone.

She considered carefully. "George…" Even telling him about Alard's news of Carina's adoption was a threat to their friendship. The information would certainly tarnish the way George viewed her. Then again, she shouldn't care so much.

"Alard told me I'm adopted," she said finally, waiting in vain for a reaction. She went on. "He says our maman et papa took me in from a society lady." She choked out a deep, croaking whisper of shame, "He said I'm…illegitimate." She pursed her lips and let the silence fall between them, knowing he was processing the shock of her words. Maybe he'd never speak to her again. Maybe, he'd…

George cleared his throat. "Your Aunt Penelope—Liam's deceased wife—was my mother."

The weight of his words dropped on her like a slap. "What?"

He nodded. "It's why Liam and I are so close. My mother, Penelope, gave birth to me out of wedlock. I was fourteen when my mother moved here from Back East. She got me a job working as a cowboy on this ranch. Then she fell in love with your Uncle Liam. She told him the truth about me, and when they got married, they agreed to treat me as a hired hand in public, so no one would know I was a…" He cleared his throat. "But they both treated me as a son in private. No one here knows Penelope was my mother, and I never knew my real father."

She knew what he didn't dare to say. *Bastard.* She swallowed hard. "I'm so sorry, George, for the loss of your mother. And your father."

He let out a frayed, worn-out breath. "Yes, I miss her a lot, but Liam has been like a father to me."

Marrin nodded. "I see." It all made sense now.

"He was ashamed to adopt me as a son, but he ended up treating me like one anyhow." There was a slight upturn to one side of his mouth. "I'm sorry you didn't feel loved by your adopted parents, Carina. It might be worse than the death of a mother."

But I did lose my mother! And my father too! And I

knew them and loved them—and they loved me! she yearned to cry out. "It's all right," said Marrin, swiping a tear that trickled down her cheek. "Maybe I said too much."

"No. Helps me understand you a little better." With lie upon lie, he really didn't know or understand her at all. "Makes sense why Liam took you in, Carina. Probably guessed his sister wasn't treating you well."

"But Uncle Liam is not my real flesh and blood uncle," Marrin whispered. "Why would he accept me at all?"

George shrugged. "Maybe he doesn't know."

More than ever, there was a part of Marrin that longed to open up to George and tell him the whole truth—that she knew what it was like to be an orphan. That she'd been forced to live with an awful aunt and uncle. That she'd felt abandoned and unloved and forced to work as a servant and cook in her own family's home. Another tear spilled from an eye, and she brushed it away.

"I'm sorry for your loss, George," she said.

"I'm sorry for yours, too, Carina."

Back at Greenwind Ranch, Liam was working in his study, Edith was cooking in the kitchen, George went back to his chores, and Alard was in his room. Nothing was out of the ordinary. Marrin went straight to her room and thoroughly searched for the missing letter. It was nowhere.

Finally, kicking off her boots and fighting sobs of dread, she fell onto her bed, awash with a mixture of relief that Liam probably didn't know the truth about her yet, but still afraid of what he might do if he did find and read the letter. Overcome with emotional fatigue, she slept fitfully.

A knock startled her, and she glanced at her clock. Nearly six in the evening already!

"Your uncle insists that you dine with him this evening, Carina," said Edith through the door.

"Yes, thank you, Edith," Marrin said heavily. "I will be there." She dreaded suppertime. She absolutely must be more careful with everything she does and everything she says. It was very possible Alard had found and read her letter, and he'd try to trap her or expose her publicly.

After changing into a suitable dress, Marrin went downstairs to join the men in the dining room. She was the last to arrive, and both Liam and George stood for her as she entered. Alard remained seated, and Liam tapped him on the shoulder. Grunting a protest, he rose and shoved himself back into his chair as Marrin made a curtsy.

"Sorry," she muttered.

Liam said a prayer aloud and launched into questioning Marrin about her first days at school. Her neck and shoulders clenched with anxiety, and her voice was small as she gave curt answers. To make matters worse, she was clumsier than usual. She dropped the saltshaker, spilled her water glass, and hit her forehead on the table when she bent to retrieve her napkin from the floor. All this as she explained how she was learning English more quickly and making friends. She still wouldn't mention her time in the corner on her first day.

"Really, Carina," said Alard, "you are a blundering dolt this evening."

"Alard, I will abide no rudeness in this house," Liam reprimanded.

"Well, it's true," he argued. "And, Carina, what was that whole curtsy thing?" She ignored him as she felt the fire in her cheeks. Why would he focus on such a small thing when he could pull out her letter and reveal its guilty contents to everyone at the table—if he'd indeed found the letter? "Bobbing like a little maid, Carina?" Alard pushed, snorting loudly.

"Alard tells me you used to ride horses," said Liam, changing the subject. "Even says you were a good rider once."

Perfect. Alard had set this trap. "That's somewhat true, Uncle Liam," said Marrin, feeling the crashing rush of her pulse in her ears. What lie could she invent now?

"Somewhat?" asked Liam.

"I did ride, but not as well as Alard recalls. I had a bad fall, and I have been afraid of horses ever since. Alard also doesn't remember that I've always been clumsy."

"Not true," said Alard. "I recall you were always nimbler than I was." His eyes pierced hers, and she jerked her gaze down to her plate. He was suspicious, for sure. "Should I share more about you and your past with Liam and George?" He asked Marrin.

The room swam and spun till she felt she might be sick.

"That's enough, Alard," Liam ordered firmly.

Alard's chest shook as he grunted and shoveled a heaping spoonful of mashed potatoes into his mouth. He took a swig of his glass of wine and set it back on the table, clinking it on the rim of his plate. "Carina," he said slowly, "what was the name of your horse back home in Belgium?"

Marrin's insides clenched. "I'm not speaking to you, Alard," she said, her throat tense and dry.

"What was the name of our governess?" Alard pressed again.

"Enough," Liam commanded hotly. "One would think you don't believe Carina is who she says she is."

"That's because…*she's not*," said Alard deliberately, menacingly.

"Uncle Liam, may I please be excused?" Marrin asked faintly.

Marrin was allowed to forego dessert and retire for the evening, but even if she hadn't received Liam's permission, she would have left the dining room anyhow.

She bade everyone good night and did her best to exit without stumbling and fainting before dragging herself upstairs to the landing, where she leaned against a wall and hauled in large, choking breaths of air.

A pounding on the staircase roused her as Alard leaped up the stairs two at a time, rushing at her in full force. Heart in her throat, she yelped and ran to her room. Grabbing the doorknob, she vaulted inside and twisted to shut the door in Alard's face. But it was too late. He clapped a hand over her mouth, shoved himself into the room with her, and slammed the door behind them.

CHAPTER 15:
Caught

"It is better to deserve honors and not have them than to have them and not deserve them."
—Mark Twain, *Notebook*, c. 1882

"*Who* are you?" Alard demanded, removing his hand from Marrin's mouth. "And don't try to scream. I need answers, and you'll start talking now."

"Alard, you're scaring me." The words shook as they panted from her mouth. She nearly fell onto the bed as her knees buckled. "And please speak in French. I do not speak good English yet."

Alard switched languages. "Maman et Papa always called you *Blue Eyes* when you were a small girl, and your eyes are brown."

So that was it? It wasn't about the letter? He must not have found it, after all. "Blue eyes?" she repeated numbly. "I don't remember that."

"You were probably too little to remember, but I do." He snorted. "I mean *Carina* was probably too little to remember. *You* wouldn't remember because you're *not* Carina."

Marrin rolled her eyes in an attempt to behave calmly

and continue her charade. "Why would Maman et Papa call me *Blue Eyes* when my eyes are brown? It makes no sense."

"Don't try to change the subject. The fact is, you *can't* be Carina. A person's eyes don't change from blue to brown."

"Alard, you're acting crazy, and it's scaring me. I *am* Carina, my eyes have always been brown, I don't remember ever being called *Blue Eyes,* and—"

"—and Carina's hair was always straight, not all…" He waved and twirled his fingers about his head. "…all curly like yours."

"Well, that's something you are right about," said Marrin. "My hair used to be straight, and now it's a little…wavy. Apparently, it happens to some people." She hauled in a breath in a prolonged attempt to regain her confidence and composure. "Alard, you had wavy hair when you were younger, didn't you?" She was really going out on a limb.

He startled. "I guess I did." He paused. "But your eyes…"

"Alard, what has gotten into you? Why are you acting so suspicious?"

She paused and frowned. "You said I'm unrelated. Maybe they wished I was someone else—someone with blue eyes."

"Just forget it, Rina," said Alard.

"Don't call me—"

"I know," he barked as he stepped to the door. "Don't call you *Rina.*"

She smiled shakily. "Exactly."

"Carina?"

"Yes?"

"No need to mention this little misunderstanding to Uncle Liam, right?"

She didn't know how to respond. She nodded, forcing a calm she didn't feel. Let him stew in his doubt—it was the only weapon she had left.

As soon as Alard left the room, she cracked into silent tears again, not sure how she felt or how she should feel. All the hiding and deception were almost more than she could take. She was so lost in lies and secrets that she was forgetting what was true and who she really was.

But she couldn't think about that. There was still the issue of the missing letter. If Alard hadn't found it, where had it gone?

Saturday's noonday sun was bright and sultry-warm, its rays glistening like crystals on the ranch pond, blinding Marrin where she sat on the wraparound porch. She sipped mint iced tea between stuttering attempts at reading aloud from a children's book loaned to her by Miss Trimble.

Marrin had slept in late that morning and was enjoying some much-needed rejuvenation after the upsetting events of the last few days. She told herself to enjoy the sunshine and the peace, to let the warmth chase away the shadows. But the weight of Alard's questioning mistrust and the still missing letter clung heavily to her shoulders.

"*Chicken Little*?" asked George, tapping the book on Marrin's lap and making her jump so she nearly spilled her tea. "Will you read me a story, Carina?"

"Don't make fun," she protested, wrinkling her nose. "Miss Trimble says reading books for children will help me learn English." George settled into a chair beside her and propped his feet on a wooden stump. "I tried to read *Tom Sawyer* and *Huckleberry Finn*," she confessed.

"You're not ready for Tom or Huck yet," George said, chuckling. "But you can read me your children's story. *The sky is falling*!" he said, waving his hands in the air. She choked back a giggle. "Please start at the beginning."

Marrin closed the book and slowly, reluctantly

reopened it at the beginning. She took a deep breath… "One day, Henny Penny was picking up corn in the rickyard—" She paused and frowned. English was so complicated to learn. "What is a rickyard?"

"Probably a chicken yard," George admitted. "It's British English."

She cleared her throat and continued reading. "Whack!" she went on reading. "An acorn hit her upon the head. 'Goodness gracious me!' said Henny Penny, 'the sky's a-going to fall; I must go and tell the King.'"

"Speaking of kings…" It was Alard disrupting their brief serenity. Marrin snapped the book shut as he sauntered across the porch to join them, dropping himself onto another chair and propping his feet on another wooden stump. "Who's the king of Belgium, Carina?"

She couldn't remember! "Who cares? You interrupt my important studies."

"You're reading a child's book about a chicken," Alard said jeeringly.

"Our dear King Leopold probably heard the same story when he was a child," Marrin said with a wink to George, jittery with excited relief at having the name of Belgium's monarch pop into her head.

Alard grunted.

"Go ahead and read, Carina," said George.

She did so with no more interruptions. Mainly because Alard got bored and went into the house after she'd read only a page, leaving her to wonder when she could get back into his room again. He clearly hadn't found her letter to Carina, but she wanted some criminal evidence about Alard so that she could send him away.

Near the end of the story, Marrin tired and wanted to stop reading, but George exhorted her to finish. "You're doing well, Carina. Your pronunciation is really good. Are you understanding most of it?"

"I think so." She let out an exasperated groan. "But the

names in child stories are so fun: Henny Penny, Rooster Booster, Foxy-woxy, Turkey-lurkey, Goosey-poosey."

"Fun-*ny*, you mean."

"Oh, yes, I mean *funny*," she repeated.

"Your English is really improving," said George.

"Thank you," she said, trying not to smile and appear too proud. But she reveled in the praise.

"Have a seat, both of you," Liam instructed Marrin and Alard after supper that evening. They seated themselves in two plush chairs opposite Mr. Stinson's desk. The early evening sun was low in the sky and flooded the interior of the room with a golden, dusty light.

"How has your Saturday been, Carina?" asked Liam.

"It was funny," she replied. "I read an entire book for children in English."

A smile twinkled in Mr. Stinson's eyes. "*Fun*, not funny," he corrected.

"Oh, dear. Those words trick me every time," she said, flustered.

"She reads a baby book and acts like it's *War and Peace*," Alard said with a sneer.

"Alard, you forget that I don't allow ridicule or hostility under my roof."

"He forgets a lot of things," Marrin said barely above a whisper.

"But I don't forget how to mail a letter," Alard said under his breath. Her body felt suddenly cold, and the smug grin on his face revealed the awful truth. "Seek and ye shall find," he whispered, leaning closer to her ear. "Marrin."

So, he'd found it! He must have gone into her room. Why hadn't she locked it? Or maybe he'd found it in the barn? He didn't seem to know about the letter the day before. She avoided meeting his piercing gaze.

"Now, may I address the kerfuffle at last night's dinner?" Liam asked, snapping Marrin out of her racing thoughts. "What was happening between you two?"

"Fuffle?" she echoed as waves of nausea set her mind spinning. How could she pay attention to Liam at a time like this?

"Our disagreement during dinner," Alard reminded her. "I thought I noticed some things about Carina that were different, Uncle, but I stand corrected."

Marrin cast her attention to Alard. He would never readily admit a mistake. He had changed tactics. What was he up to?

"What sorts of things did you notice, Alard?" Liam asked. Marrin's heart tightened.

"Just that I thought I remembered Maman et Papa calling her *Blue Eyes* when she was little, but why would they do that if her eyes are brown?"

Liam picked up a silver frame containing a photo of Alard and Carina with their parents. "You can't tell in a photograph."

Marrin was too afraid to speak for a moment. "That reminds me of another disagreement Alard and I had, Uncle Liam," Marrin ventured.

"What's that?" Liam asked, replacing the photograph on a shelf near his desk.

"I told Carina about being adopted," Alard spat out. "Apparently, Maman and Papa never told her."

"What?" Liam gasped.

"I'm sure you know. The society lady who had a child out of wedlock and gave her to Maman to care for."

"Alard!" Liam nearly shouted, his neck so taut, the veins stood out. "How could you say such a thing?"

"I guess you didn't know," said Alard, squinting.

"I'm sure it's a lie," said Liam. "Carina, don't listen to him."

Marrin nodded, wide-eyed at his reaction.

"You can ask Maman yourself," said Alard. "She's the one who told me."

"Preposterous!" Liam spluttered.

"Write to her," Alard urged. "And ask her about Carina's eyes, too, while you're at it. Prove I'm not completely crazy and forgetful."

Oh, dear. If Liam sent a letter to Alard's mother asking about her eye color, it would set the clock to ticking. But it was already ticking now that Carina's brother had read her letter.

"It's been a long day, and I need rest," Alard said abruptly, excusing himself to retire for the evening.

Carina was left alone with Liam in his study. He leaned back in his chair as a frown bunched the space between his eyes. "Carina, do you feel at home here?"

She swallowed over a lump in her throat. She sensed the tenderness in his sympathetic tone more than the words he spoke. "I do, but could Alard be right? I mean, if I am adopted, it might explain why Maman et Papa never liked me. But it could also mean that I'm not related to you at all."

"I'll look into it, Carina, but I don't believe you were adopted. Complete nonsense." His expression was one of disgust and annoyance. "I can see why you dislike Alard."

"What should I do? Should I stay?"

"I'd like you to stay." His eyes twinkled a little. "Maybe you'll even fall in love." Marrin felt the pink in her cheeks.

A smile that lay hidden behind his mustache. "I've seen how you've obeyed my orders regarding George, but I also see how neither of you can hide your feelings for one another."

"Oh, no! We are only friends, Uncle Liam, really."

He raised an eyebrow. "There's no shame in liking him. He's a good fellow."

"I know, but you forbade me from…how do you say? Encourage him? And I do my best."

Liam chuffed lightly. "He asked to court you, Carina. I said no, but I've had my eye on you two."

"Oh, dear. I…I…I'm sorry he asked you that."

Mr. Stinson leaned forward, resting his forearms on his desk. "I told him to wait and allow you to settle into your new home and school before he approaches you. You have a lot of adjustments to make in a new country, getting to know me and other people here. I want you to focus on your education and make new friends before you get distracted with courting just yet." She noticed her mouth had dropped open and snapped it shut. "Do you agree with me, Carina?"

"Yes, of course. As I said, Uncle Liam, I only think of George as a friend."

His eyebrows traveled up his forehead, and he looked as though he did not believe her. "Good." He glanced at a clock on the fireplace mantel. "It's getting late. You've had rather a trying day with your brother telling you such astonishing things, and there's church in the morning. I suggest you get some sleep."

Marrin bade Liam good night and was about to leave the study when she stopped and faced him. "Uncle Liam," she asked tentatively, "may I kiss you good night?" His face reddened, and he seemed unable to give an answer. He ducked his head shyly and began cleaning his spectacles with a handkerchief.

Marrin stepped over, brushed his cheek with a quick kiss, and left the room. It might be the last time he'd ever regard her fondly before Alard told him the truth. Greenwind Ranch had begun to feel like home, and Liam had started to feel like family. Guilt stabbed at her heart at the thought of how she had deceived such a kind, loving, fatherly gentleman. And she was deceiving George, too.

As she tiptoed up the stairs and sped past Alard's bedroom door, she wondered if she should confront Alard now? No, she was too exhausted emotionally. But she had to break the news to Mr. Stinson before Alard did. When was the best time and opportunity to do that?

She let out a deep breath as she closed her bedroom door and turned the key in the lock. If Alard told the truth about her, it would ruin everything—all her hopes, all her plans. She needed to take the money she had and somehow make it back to France to rescue her little sister. They could start a new life together. Perhaps they'd even return to America someday.

She wriggled beneath the light summer quilt on her comfortable bed and watched the pale moonlight dance on the ceiling through her lace curtains. She hadn't felt so loved, so cherished, so cared for in years—and she craved it with all her soul. Liam Stinson was the family and father she'd longed for since her parents passed away.

She hiccupped over a sob. The thought of leaving this pretend family was more than she could bear. She wanted to remain Carina Lejeune and stay at Greenwind Ranch forever. But she knew Alard was about to destroy her life.

CHAPTER 16:
A Gathering Storm

"He had a secret which he was burning to tell but dared not." –Mark Twain, *Tom Sawyer*

"Enjoy your time at church," Alard said, his grin too knowing, his eyes flicking to Marrin with a gleam of something unspoken as he lounged on the front porch, feet on a log stump, smoking a cigar.

"Wish you'd come with us, Alard," said Liam, his voice strained.

"A man needs a *real* Sabbath rest now and then, Uncle," said Alard. "Sunday's my rest day."

"A rest from what?" Liam muttered beneath his breath. Both Marrin and George exchanged glances. Alard didn't do much to help around the ranch, and everyone knew it.

After helping Marrin into the backseat of the surrey to sit beside Liam, George climbed into the driver's seat, and they headed into town to St. Mark's.

"Uncle Liam," Marrin spoke up after a time, "would you like me to help you around the ranch? I could help Edith in the kitchen or help her clean the house if you'd like."

A smile creased his face. "You heard the tone of my remark about your lazy brother?" She sucked her lower lip between her teeth. "I oughtn't to have said that, Carina. I just wish Alard would offer to assist around the place in exchange for room and board. You, on the other hand, are a most welcome guest. You're studious, unobtrusive, and continuously full of gratitude. A joy to have around."

"Thank you, Uncle Liam," she said, blushing at the compliments.

Upon arrival, they were warmly greeted by several folks, including Collette and Milly, who tittered shyly behind their hands and tried to make eye contact with George and other older boys. Marrin and her friends shared a pew, and the three girls scribbled notes during the service.

Milly nudged Marrin and passed a note: *Does George like any girls?*

Marrin scribbled: *Maybe... I won't say.*

Collette peeked over: *You?*

Marrin shook her head, heat rising to her neck. A fly buzzed past the golden light of the oil-papered windows, and she ducked her head, slipping the note back.

A wink from George across the pew made her heart skip. Milly's note followed: *He likes you!!!* Marrin groaned silently.

The girls stifled giggles as the congregation rose for the doxology. Marrin sang in French, comforted by the familiar tune.

I have to focus, she reminded herself. Thoughts of George would wait.

Near the close of the service, Collette gulped a snort as she slid a heart-decorated note to Marrin with the words, *Je t'aime* written on it, and Milly and Collette's giggles became more pronounced.

The nave erupted with the creaking of wooden pews as the congregation rose for the doxology. Marrin sang along in French while everyone else sang the words in English. It was a comfort to recognize the tune.

"I think you like him too," Collette whispered to Marrin as the hymn ended.

Marrin didn't answer. Thoughts buzzed in her head. It was wonderful to know George liked her, and maybe she did like him back. But none of that mattered now. She had to either escape and let Alard spill the truth about her or somehow break the news to Liam herself.

"Do you like George?" Collette asked too loudly as they shuffled out of the church to stand within the confines of the picket fence separating the narrow churchyard from the street.

"Sh!" said Marrin. "Not so loud."

"But I'm speaking French," Collette persisted.

"*He* can speak French," Marrin hissed, tilting her head toward George.

"Oh, là là," said Collette. "Isn't that nice?"

"No, it's not," said Marrin, pinning a stern eye on her new friend.

"But do you like him?"

"Absolutely not," said Marrin.

Collette tossed her bouncy ringlets. "If you can't see that you like George, you deceive yourself." George waved just then, beckoning for Marrin to return to the surrey. "I think he wants you," Collette added, teasingly.

Marrin said goodbye to Collette and Milly, allowing George to take her hand as he assisted her into the surrey. And, though both George and Liam attempted conversation with her on the ride home, her mind was fractured, scattered. She decided she wouldn't let Alard snitch on her. She was going to get her letter back and destroy it.

Alard was civil at lunch. Suspiciously so. Marrin didn't trust it. Not after the way his eyes lingered too long on her face, threatening her with silent knowing. She had to get back into Alard's room to search for that letter.

But Alard didn't leave his room after lunch. She sat on the back porch in the hot, sultry stillness of the afternoon, legs crossed, one foot swinging nervously beneath her skirt as she watched the billow of thunderheads gather on the horizon, and the pasture pond darken to a deep blue gray.

She pictured it: the clink of saddle buckles, the scrape of a bag tied hastily to Pinto's flank, the frantic rhythm of hooves as she galloped down the road to the station and boarded a train headed east. If she couldn't get that letter back from Alard, she needed a more concrete plan.

The wind shuddered a ripple of waves across the water, slipping around her body in a current of eerie coolness while the horizon stretched with distant curtains of rain.

Once she returned to Amiens, she'd have to stay in a hotel and somehow wait for a chance to slip into her aunt and uncle's house, steal her sister away, and leave town. To be truly safe, she and Robinette should return to America. Maybe they could find a place to live in the Midwestern States. Or maybe Texas. But all this would cost a great deal of money—more than she'd already stolen from Alard.

"I've been watching you, Rina," a caustic voice spoke, shattering her scheming thoughts. She stilled the anxious bouncing of her foot beneath her skirt. There was something wrong with Alard's manner. "I can see the wheels in your brain turning." He hissed a sinister chuckle as he shuffled across the porch. *A cold shiver ran down her spine, and* her knees nearly gave way as her eyes caught the white corner of a paper peeking from his shirt pocket—an envelope!

Lightning flashed, and the breeze stiffened. She stood on shaking legs. "A storm is coming. I'm going inside."

"Why don't we go for a walk, Carina?" Alard crushed the butt of his cigar on the porch rail.

She shook her head. "You can walk by yourself."

He stretched and yawned. "Oh, I think you'll walk with me," he said casually, pulling the envelope from his pocket. She recognized her penmanship and the name: *Carina Lejeune.*

A cold shiver ran through her as Alard's words cut the air. She stumbled backward, catching herself on the grass, heart hammering.

"Let's talk," he said, nearly losing the envelope in a gust of wind before he replaced it in his pocket. He gestured beyond the porch steps to the path winding to the pond.

As though moving in slow-motion through a thick fog, she turned and stepped as lightly as possible down the steps, gripping the rail for support as the wind wrapped her skirt around her shins. She felt faint. Should she allow herself to faint? Would anyone come to her aid? No, she mustn't faint. Maybe she should run back into the house and confess everything to Liam now, before Alard got to him and gave him a tainted, imperfect, impure version of her story….

"Who are you, exactly?" Alard demanded. Marrin jerked away from him and turned to run back up the path to the house, but Alard jumped, gripped her upper arm, and squeezed it until she yelped with pain. "Oh, no, I'm not letting you get away, missy," he barked, pulling her further down the path to a grove of cottonwood trees along the water's edge.

Thunder rumbled again, and a blast of wind struck them in a swirl of dust mixed with the first droplets of rain. "You're hurting me," she whimpered.

"Don't care," he shouted above the gale. "Tell me who you are and what's happened to my sister."

Head spinning, aching, Marrin tried to think of how to tell him as little as possible before she could escape and confess everything to Liam.

"Tell me who you are, *Marrin*," Alard spat out the name, beads of saliva raining onto her cheeks. *The way he spoke her real name cut like a blade, slicing the air—and her breath—with it.*

Marrin gasped, wrenching her skirt from his grasp. Her legs trembled, heart hammering. "Answer me!" he shouted.

"I can't!" she cried. "You're hurting me." Tears ran down her cheeks as her shoulders quivered.

"Here's the situation," he said menacingly. "I don't

know who you are. You look a lot like Carina, but you are *not* my sister. From your letter, you made some sort of arrangement with my sister. You're an imposter living under my uncle's roof, eating his food, wearing his late wife's clothes, living the life of a pampered princess." He shook the envelope in the air. "Tell me everything." Marrin's teeth rattled as she stepped back, trying to catch her breath.

"I'll get the truth out of you eventually. I've thought of several things I could do to you. I could tell Uncle Liam and have you sent away. I could turn you into the sheriff and have you put in jail. I could have you deported back to France." He paced back and forth through the tall, clumpy grass before stopping to face her squarely. "But I've decided not to do any of these things. Not yet anyhow," he added. "You want to know why?" She nodded numbly. "You'll do as I say," he said, eyes narrowing. "Refuse me, and there'll be consequences you wouldn't want anyone to hear about."

"I don't have any money—" she began, her voice shuddering.

"You're going to pay me the way a woman pays a man," he sneered with a grumble beneath his breath.

"I don't understand," she stammered. She couldn't comprehend what he was saying. "I can't pay you. I don't know how to get money to pay you."

"Don't play innocent with me." His eyes narrowed as he scanned her body, and her nerves gripped with fear as her knees banged against each other. "Only a worldly girl would have the nerve to play the games you're playing. You and my sister." He coughed up a laugh. "You wrote to Carina that you suspect I'm a criminal outlaw. Ain't that callin' the kettle black?" She didn't understand his English slang. "Here are a few options," Alard went on. "You could service me alone, but I can't stand how much you look like my own sister—and others think you're my sister, so it would be more profitable for me to get you a job in a house of a certain reputation in Yreka. Kill a few birds with one stone."

An inky, cold darkness in his words closed around her throat. He didn't mean a house of ill repute, did he? She opened her mouth and spoke through clicking teeth, "I refuse to listen to any more of your foolishness, Alard!" she chattered shakily.

"You *refuse*?" he asked, his tone mocking. "Unless you want to disappoint and shame my Uncle Liam, you'll do exactly as I tell you. Oh, and I did a little research on the exact nature of your crimes. In these parts, you're what the authorities call a *confidence* woman." He nodded impressively. "That's right. The law in this country states that lying to people in order to persuade them to give you their money or property is a serious crime. A crime of fraud punishable by a hefty prison sentence."

Marrin's knees gave out beneath her, and she stumbled, lurching sideways, nearly collapsing. How could she ever help her little sister if she were in prison? Alard was right. The word "criminal" echoed in her mind like a curse. Her chest tightened, breath shallow, guilt sucking air from her lungs. But if he was suggesting that she work as a prostitute, that was worse than a prison sentence.

"Oh, and, if a judge is angry enough," Alard added, "he'll have you hanged."

Marrin's vision blurred, and she crumpled to the ground. Alard's voice kept on, but the volume muffled and faded. The hard sting of a slap on her cheek woke her, and she opened her eyes to blink up at Alard's toothy smile as he pressed her head into a clump of wet grass. Shoving her clawing fingernails into Alard's face, she caught him off guard for the split second she needed to drag herself across the ground and away from the repulsive man.

"Get up," Alard seethed. "George is coming, and if you know what's good for you, you'll get up and act normal. Say you fell because you're so blamed clumsy." She pushed herself up to a seated position but was unable to stand. "Just remember there's no hope for you, Mademoiselle Marrin. You either work for me and do as I say, or it's jail for you."

"No!" The word scratched like grit from her parched lips.

"You don't have a choice," Alard mumbled while George was still several yards away. "Hello, there!" Alard shouted. "I have some startling news to give you and Uncle Liam."

"No, please!" Marrin cried. "Don't say anything. Not yet."

"What news?" George called out.

"It's about this little wench," said Alard.

"Alard, please!" Marrin hissed.

"What happened?" asked George, hurrying to Marrin's side and extending his hand to help her up.

"She's not who she claims to be," Alard went on.

"Are you all right, Carina?" asked George, ignoring Alard. "What happened? Did you fall?" He wrapped his arm around her waist and tugged her against his side as he pulled her to her feet.

"The girl's a fraud, George."

"Alard, not now," said George, clearly annoyed. "It's clear the two of you dislike each other, but you're cruel to leave her on the ground and not offer any help to your own sister."

"She's not my sister."

George grunted. "Must you always be so insufferable? What is it with you two?" Marrin's fingers trembled as she smoothed her skirt and leaned slightly on George's arm, absorbing a little of his strength.

"I'll tell you exactly what it is, George."

"Not now," he spat back again, his response clipped and commanding. "A storm's brewing. I'll take Carina back to the house." Keeping his arm around her, George steadied Marrin as they walked.

"The wretched girl is an imposter, George!" Alard

called out. "A complete fraud. And I can prove it." George made no reply. "Hours are all you have, Carina," Alard yelled. "You have till tomorrow morning to decide what to do. Hours before I tell Liam everything."

"Ignore him," George said, his breath and lips warm and comforting on her ear.

"He is acting crazy," whispered Marrin as the drops of rain grew larger and dampened her hair.

"You've got that right," he replied as Alard continued to scream rash, angry threats behind them.

"I'm scared, George," said Marrin unsteadily, her volume low.

"Forget about him, Carina."

"I have proof she's not who she says she is, George!" Alard shouted, his voice whipping away in the rising wind.

Marrin stopped and spun round. Raindrops like bullets struck her face, and Alard stood waving the incriminating letter in the air.

"Please, God," she begged, her lips trembling. "Let the wind take it. Let it vanish." But the wind betrayed her. Alard stood laughing hysterically at her as he tucked the envelope back into his pocket and began jogging toward them. Gripping George's arm, Marrin turned and increased her speed. "Hurry!" she panted. "He frightens me."

"If you're that afraid of him, Carina, I'll talk to your uncle and have him thrown out of the house."

Yes—get him thrown out. That would be—No. No, that was worse. He'd retaliate. He'd tell everything, and she'd go to jail or prison. Marrin and George climbed the porch steps.

No, she'd have to steal that letter from Alard and destroy it before he could show it to anyone. Then maybe she'd be able to prove the man was insane.

Marrin limped into the house just ahead of George as he slammed the door behind them. Turning back, she viewed Alard through the small window in the door. He approached the steps, his fierce dark eyes catching hers with alarming ferocity. He patted his shirt pocket and leered.

"Marrin, go upstairs and get ready for supper," George commanded gruffly. "Let me talk to your brother."

Lightning flashed, and a crash of thunder shook the house, rattling pictures on the walls as Alard burst through the door.

"Please, Alard," she begged.

"I hold all the power, Carina." The words whistled through Alard's teeth. "Do we have an agreement?"

"Yes," she nodded.

"Good." Alard's tone shifted in an instant—calm, smooth, almost amused as if none of the venom from moments earlier had ever existed. He slapped George on the shoulder. "Quite a storm out there, George. Join me for a whisky before supper?"

Marrin stumbled up the stairs to her room and vomited into the chamber pot. She washed her mouth and face in fresh water from the pitcher and basin and lightly touched the red splotch on her cheek where Alard had struck her. The walls crackled in another roll of thunder, and she no longer tried to choke back sobs that came in heaves as she sank onto the bed. "What should I do, God?" she prayed. Tears slid down her cheeks. "I don't know if You're real, but if You are, I need Your help now."

She heaved herself up and sat listening on the edge of her mattress, straining her ears. The sound of George and Alard's conversation downstairs in the parlor was sprinkled with laughter. If she couldn't get that letter back from Alard, she'd have to steal more money from Alard's room and make her escape. Now!

Tiptoeing into Alard's room, Marrin shut the door and tore into where she'd found Alard's hidden money before. But it was gone. She searched the entire room to find only sixty dollars in one of Alard's socks. Sixty dollars was better than nothing, so she took it, returning to her own room just as she heard Alard's heavy footfall ascending the stairs. Heart pounding, she locked the door behind her back, panting to catch her breath before flying to the armoire to grab a dress and warm coat, which she crammed into a satchel. The stolen sixty dollars joined the other stash of bills she'd stuffed into the bottom of the bag, where the lining had torn and formed a sort of pocket. She selected one of Aunt Penelope's humble calico dresses to wear to school the following morning, draping it over the foot of the brass bed.

Flashes of light broke into the room, and she sat at the desk to pen a note to Alard:

Alard, please wait. We have an agreement.

She had no intention of doing what he demanded. Her note to him was to distract him, stall him until she was able to leave town. She'd depart from school at eleven the following morning and be on the noon train headed to Canada and the French-speaking province of Quebec. That was her new plan. She'd use Alard's money to rent a flat and find work. Someday, she'd make enough to return to France, where she'd steal away her little sister and take her somewhere safe.

She added a second line to her note:

Meet me in the barn after school on Monday to discuss work in Yreka.

She shuddered as she folded the sheet of stationery and stuffed it into an envelope; then she sealed it and scrawled Alard's name on the outside. She hated that Alard would think she had intentions of giving in to his disgusting proposal.

Lightning splintered the gloom again, and thunder rattled the windowpanes as Marrin scribbled furiously. *I am Marrin Fournier, not Carina Lejeune… Alard must never see this.* She paused, thinking through the rest of her escape plan. *He'll ruin everything.* Biting her lip, she added only what Liam and George needed to know, leaving out anything Alard could twist against her.

She enclosed the contract she and Carina had signed and sealed the envelope, kissing it lightly. *This must be enough to explain everything—before Alard can.*

A tear spilled from her eye and landed on the page, smudging George's surname. She blotted the paper and carefully slid the letter into an envelope, sealing it and kissing it tenderly while gulping back more tears. There was no time or space for crying now. Once she was on the train, she'd walk to the caboose and stand outside on the tiny porch at the back and cry where no one could hear or see her. She couldn't think of that now, or she'd weep uncontrollably and be unable to think clearly.

Marrin stood and walked to the door, pressing her ear to the wooden panel. George and Alard's gruff, throaty conversation continued. She crept to Alard's room one more time.

Lighting flashed, and she whirled round just as Alard opened the door. Sucking in her breath, she placed a finger to her lips and took a shaky step toward him.

Thunder echoed and shook the walls. "I came to give you this," she said hoarsely, pointing to the note she'd placed on his desk. "You're welcome." She tried to skirt past him; then she darted for the door. But his fingers entwined in her skirt and jerked her back.

"Let go of me!" she cried, wrenching her skirt from his grasp. She nearly fell through the doorway onto the balcony before slamming the door in Alard's face. Stumbling backward, she lost her balance and fell against the railing, barely missing the stairs as George bounded to steady her.

"Carina?" he asked, his whispered breath cool on her cheek. "Did he try to hurt you?"

"I…I don't know," Marrin panted. Lightning flickered as she glanced warily at Alard's bedroom door. If he came out now, he might tell George everything. But he did not emerge. She pulled away from George and took a halting step toward her bedroom.

"Are you sure you're all right?" George asked, moving closer.

She nodded. "He frightened me, but I'll be fine. I'm just tired. I need to sleep."

"But you'll miss supper."

"I'm fine," she said. "It has been a difficult day for me. I need sleep."

"I'll bring you something to eat."

"No, that would not be proper," she protested, her voice soft.

"Then I'll have Edith bring you something."

Marrin nodded, turned, and leaned against the outside of her bedroom door. Facing George, she sucked in her breath and fought a sob that stuck in her throat. Soon, she'd never see this man again. The thought tore at her heart, and she spun round, slipped into her room, and closed the door as she mouthed a quick word of thanks to him.

A golden glow of sunset shone through the breaking storm, casting light upon the letter she'd written to Liam and George. It lay on the desk like a death sentence. This would be her last night at Greenwind Ranch. If she didn't see Liam Stinson the following morning before school, she might never see him again. She couldn't bear the loss, but she had no choice. The words of her letter would break his heart, but the pain had to come sooner or later. If only Alard hadn't arrived. But that wouldn't have made things any easier. She was destined to cause these good people pain, no matter what she did.

She shoved a few more essentials into her satchel and changed into her nightgown. She'd lie to George the next morning and say she needed the bag for sharing some things from Belgium with her classmates.

More lies. Always lies. But tomorrow the lies would end. Tomorrow she'd be far, far from this lovely place and these dear people. She'd never forget them. She'd always love them. All of them. She inhaled sharply.

Even George.

Especially George.

And she felt something. Something so strange, new, and different, she wondered if it might be love. But she wasn't sure.

CHAPTER 17:
Escape

"The secret of getting ahead is getting started." —
from Mark Twain's *Notebook*

𝒜 knock pounded at the door, dragging Marrin from a restless sleep. Yawning, she thought she was dreaming until she heard the sound repeated. She pushed herself onto her elbows and saw that the clock beside her bed in the early morning light. It was nearly half past six.

"Carina, are you awake?" asked Edith. "Are you coming down to breakfast?"

"Yes, I'll be down soon," said Marrin, thrusting the quilt from her and placing her feet on the braided rug beside the bed. She would need to dress hastily and somehow place her farewell letter in Liam's study before the seven o'clock departure time.

She gave herself a quick sponge bath, dressed, made her bed, and rushed downstairs. Crossing through the parlor to the hallway, she crashed headlong into Alard as he stepped from behind a high-backed chair. He waved her letter in front of her nose before tucking it inside his shirt.

"I'm glad we've come to this little business arrangement, Marrin," he said, his lips stretched tightly above his teeth.

"You gave me no choice," Marrin mumbled, trying to push her way past him—and wishing she was skilled in the art of pickpocketing.

He grabbed her arm. "I'll meet you at the schoolhouse at three o'clock."

His words made her vision swim. "I can't. I said I would meet you in the barn at—"

"I know what you wrote, but I make the rules, Marrin, dear," he jeered. "Yreka is where you work now, and I need to introduce you to your new employer. I'll tell Liam and George I'll escort you home from school this afternoon."

"Fine," she agreed, yanking her arm from his grip and knowing neither would agree to that plan. Besides, she'd be gone on the noon train by the time anyone came to the schoolhouse looking for her. She edged past Alard and entered the noisy dining room, where George waved her to a seat beside him at the table. She stopped in the doorway. She'd have to get into Liam's study after breakfast to leave her letter for him.

"I'm glad you're used to being the only girl in a room full of dirty, stinking men," Alard snarled in her ear as he stood behind her. "You'll fit right in with them soon enough."

Marrin turned, slapped Alard full in the face, and the room went quiet.

George jumped to his feet. "What's going on?" he shouted. "Alard, what have you done? What did you say to her?"

"He offered to escort me home after school today," said Marrin, "and I…I don't feel comfortable being with him."

"Of course, not," said George. "I'll continue to be your sister's escort to and from school, Alard. Now that that's settled, come and eat your breakfast, Carina."

She never looked back at Alard as she took a seat beside George.

"Your hands are shaking," said George as she finished

her silent prayer and picked up a fork.

"That man is brutal, cruel, hateful—"

"Yes, yes," said George. "Take a deep breath and eat something. I'll talk to your uncle about him. I don't know what it is between you two, but he does have a bad effect on you."

Marrin pushed fried potatoes around her plate and sipped some coffee with milk. She couldn't see any way to get her letter back from Alard. "He's dreadful. Absolutely frightening," she said in her native language. She wanted to mention her suspicions that he was a thief, but was afraid to implicate herself. "He's mean, threatening—"

"Carina, mon chère," George whispered, "don't worry about him. I'll do whatever I can to protect you. I'll have him removed from this house if your uncle will hear me."

"Merci, George." George really was a good man. And he seemed to truly care for her. How she wished she could stay and be with him. They might have had a future together. "Excuse me. I have to finish getting ready," she said, sliding her chair from the table and standing.

"But you haven't finished your meal," George protested.

"I haven't time. I'll meet you in the barn." She apologized again and ducked out to hurry to Liam's office. She prayed he'd be gone—but also, somehow, wished for one last glimpse of him.

When she knocked on the door, Liam Stinson answered and asked her to enter.

"Good morning, Carina," he said, rising.

"Don't get up. I just thought I'd stop by to say good morning and goodbye to you before school. I didn't get to see you at dinner last night."

"Yes, we missed you," said Liam, sitting again.

"You're so kind," she said, choking a little on the words. She'd miss him terribly. Where could she secretly place the letter so that he wouldn't find it until later? She crossed to his desk and sat in the chair opposite him. Ah, of course. She'd place it in his Bible, which he read every evening in the parlor.

Alard still had the letter meant for Carina—the one that could ruin her. But this letter, the one tucked inside Uncle Liam's Bible, told the truth. Liam read his Bible every evening without fail. By then, she would be gone. *George wouldn't know unless Alard told him first.*

"You've been a good uncle to me," she said. "I'm so happy now that I came to live with you. I wasn't sure it was a good thing at first, but now I see it was providential."

"I agree," Liam smiled with twinkling eyes. "You've changed since you first arrived."

"How so?"

He tilted his head. "You're more part of the family." He chuckled. "And your manners have improved."

"Yes," she admitted. "When I first arrived, I forgot how to behave properly."

"I think you're delightful, my dear, and so does everyone else who comes into contact with you," said Liam. "But don't let that go to your head. I don't want you to be known as Liam Stinson's spoiled niece."

"I thank you again for all you've done for me," she said with a melancholy smile. "May I look at the photograph again—the one of me with my family when I was little?"

Liam turned his back to grab the photo frame, and Marrin took the chance to slip her letter into the Bible on the desk.

"You were a cute little thing," said Liam, handing her the photograph.

Marrin smiled, glanced at the foursome in black and white, and handed it back. Then she stood, walked around the desk, and stooped to give Mr. Stinson a quick peck on the cheek. "Goodbye and God bless you, Uncle Liam."

"Goodness, my dear," he said. "You'd think you were leaving us for good."

She hurried out and fled upstairs to grab her satchel. *Yes, Uncle Liam, leaving you is for your good.*

"You're awfully talkative this morning, Sparky. I'm happy to see you've recovered from whatever Alard did or said to you," George said gently.

Marrin wasn't recovered, but she'd decided to make these last few moments with George count, asking him questions about his life, his likes and dislikes, his mother, his grandmother in Belgium, and Liam. She wanted to remember everything she could in the short space she had left.

"Why so many questions?" he asked as they neared the schoolhouse. "You'd think you had a genuine interest in me or something."

"Or something," said Marrin with an impish perk to her lips.

Her throat was so constricted, she could barely swallow as she struggled to bid farewell to George for the last time. Her heart pounded, and she fought the impulse to give him a squeeze goodbye.

In class, she paid very little attention to her studies and nervously watched the clock as the minutes ticked closer and closer to eleven. That evening, she imagined what would happen back at the ranch. She wouldn't be at the schoolhouse when George came to fetch her. Liam Stinson would probably still take the time to read his Bible in the evening and find her letter of confession. He'd be furious. He'd show it to George, and they'd both be furious. And Alard would surely give them the letter she'd written to Carina.

It was one of the last days of school before the summer break, and during recess, Marrin hugged her new friends and told them she had to leave to run errands for her uncle in town.

"You're acting strange," said Collette. "You never hugged me goodbye before. What's wrong?"

"Nothing," she lied. "Just thinking of how we won't see each other as much over the summer."

"I think she's becoming more comfortable with hugging," said Milly, who hugged everyone all the time. How Marrin would miss these two girls.

"George does like me a little," Marrin whispered to Collette when they were alone for a moment, "and you're right that I do like him."

"I knew it!" Collette exclaimed.

"Sh!" said Marrin with a finger to her lips. "I think he will soon grow to hate me, however, so I think you should seriously consider him as a suitor for yourself, Collette."

Collette grimaced. "I could never steal your beau, silly goose."

"You can't steal something I never had," said Marrin as she mounted Pinto and waved goodbye. *George is not my beau and never will be.*

Riding into Yreka, Marrin breathed in the scent of rain-washed grass and junipers. She barely made it to Miner Street when a paper tacked to the side of a building flapped in the wind, catching her eye. She wouldn't have given it a second glance, except that the man's face sketched on the paper looked familiar—from a distance.

She halted Pinto in front of the sheriff's office, dismounted, and hopped onto the boardwalk to take a closer look at the wanted poster. *Alard Lejeune*! She gasped and tore the paper from the wall, holding it in her shaking hands. She was about to enter the building to tell the sheriff about Alard, but stopped.

If she told him now, he'd take a posse out to Greenwind

Ranch to make an arrest. Alard would tell Liam everyone her true identity, and the sheriff might arrest her before she could catch the train out of town. What should she do? Maybe she could mail the poster to Liam from another town. But, by then, it might be too late. Alard might get away.

The door suddenly opened, and the sheriff appeared in front of her, a shiny star badge pinned to his shirt. "May I help you, young lady?" he asked.

She folded the poster and tucked it into a pocket. "No, not yet," she muttered. "I…I have to do something first. I'll be back later." The poster crumpled slightly in her grip, damp with sweat.

The sheriff's brow crinkled as he pressed a hat onto his head and walked up the street.

She had to purchase her ticket first, then wait until close to boarding time before running back to the sheriff to show him the wanted poster and tell him about Alard. Then she'd hurry back, hop onto the train, and be on her way. Safe.

She spun round to head toward the train station—and nearly collided with George, who had silently crept up behind her. Startled, she jumped backward and leaned against the sheriff's office door.

"Good morning, mademoiselle," said George, gripping her wrist and pulling her off the boardwalk into the street. "Get in," he said, gesturing to Liam Stinson's surrey now parked beside Pinto.

"What?" she blinked, baffled, stunned. *This was not the George she knew.* His grip was tight, his jaw rigid—not cruel, but furious. He couldn't know yet—could he?

Her pulse thudded painfully, and she tried to play dumb. "You certainly are rude all of a sudden. What's gotten into you, George?"

"Don't toy with me," he spat angrily. "We're going home, if you can even call Greenwind your home."

CHAPTER 18:
Caught

"If you tell the truth, you don't have to remember anything." Widely attributed to Mark Twain

Marrin's chest imploded with the shock of George's words. She stood her ground. "I have not finished school for the day."

"As if you'll ever spend another day in school," he said, his fingers laced tightly around her forearm.

"What about Pinto?" she asked meekly. "We can't leave him." She glanced at her satchel on the back of the saddle—with all the money she'd stolen from Alard. "Shouldn't I ride him back?"

"You think I'd risk letting you ride Liam's horse so you could escape?" he asked derisively. "Get into the surrey, or I'll pick you up and throw you in."

"I'd like to see you try," she said, her tone miserable and cross, half afraid he might do exactly as he threatened. She yanked her arm from his grasp and climbed into the back of the vehicle as George led Pinto from the hitching post to the back of the carriage, where he tied the horse to a hook on the tailgate.

As George hauled up into the driver's seat, Marrin jumped out the other side and raced up the street, dodging pedestrians as she darted past the saloon and bakery toward the last place she'd seen the sheriff. But he had disappeared.

"Help! Help! Sheriff! Sheriff!" she called. "Where's the sheriff?" She turned to other people on the boardwalk. "Has anyone seen the sheriff?"

Someone pointed at the bank, and she plunged inside. "Sheriff!" she wheezed. "Is the sheriff in here?" Customers looked around and shook their heads as she felt George's hand squeeze her bicep. "This criminal is Alard Lejeune!" she shouted in her thick accent, waving the wanted poster in the air. "He is the nephew of Liam Stinson at Greenwind Ranch."

"Don't listen to her," said George. "This girl is a criminal herself."

"That is not true," Marrin protested as George jerked her roughly toward the door.

"If anyone does see the sheriff," George continued, "you can tell him to come out to Greenwind Ranch to arrest this lady and slap her in jail."

"This paper has a picture of the nephew of Monsieur Stinson," Marrin cried in broken English as George yanked her out the door. "He lives at Greenwind Ranch. S'il vous plaît, somebody must tell the sheriff! Alard tries to blame moi!"

A woman in the bank snatched the wanted poster from her hand as George seized her arm and hauled her struggling down the street to the surrey, slamming himself beside her. A man frowned uncertainly. A woman hesitated—but when George spoke again, their eyes slid away. No one did anything to help her as George repeated his accusations that she was a criminal and he was placing her under citizen's arrest.

"Hold on tight," George told her through gritted teeth, slapping the reins and lurching the carriage down the street.

"Please, George," Marrin begged, "you must believe me. Alard is a dangerous criminal."

"And who should I believe?" George ground out. "A lying imposter and a stranger or Liam's flesh and blood family?"

She pointed to the side of a building. "Look! Look at that poster, George. It is Alard, I promise you!"

"I've half a mind to stuff a bandana in your mouth to keep you quiet," said George, urging the team onward as they turned onto Main Street with Pinto trotting behind.

"I tell you the truth," Marrin whimpered softly, fearful her protests might provoke him to gag her.

Don't even think of using tears to soften me," he said. "I'm so goldarn infuriated with your duplicity—making us all believe you're Liam's niece. It's despicable. I'd never want to see you again, but Liam made me come to town to fetch you."

"Why?"

"He wants to hear your side of the story, although I don't know why."

"Did Alard tell you?" Marrin asked, her voice shaky.

"Yes. I sat down in the parlor to read a chapter of the Bible—something I do some mornings."

"I didn't know you did that," she muttered.

"Good thing too. I gave your letter to Liam, and he read it aloud to me. Then we read it to Alard, and he said we'd better fetch you before you tried to leave town or some such nonsense, which I believe you were about to do." He grit his teeth. "Is that about right?"

She shook her head. "No, that is not correct. First, I was planning to tell the sheriff about Alard. I saw the poster today—for the first time."

"I trusted you," George said bitterly. "And you made a fool of me."

Tears brimmed in Marrin's eyes, but she blinked them away. Tears would not help her. If only she still had that poster of Alard now. She'd shove it in his face, and he'd see the truth. But he'd know the truth eventually. The posters were probably posted everywhere. She might be in jail before Liam and George knew the truth, but she didn't care anymore. But could she be hanged for her crimes? She shuddered. She wasn't sure she cared about that anymore either. The worst thing was that George despised her.

"Why does Mr. Stinson want me to come back to the ranch? Why does he not tell the sheriff to put me in jail?"

"Liam says your letter doesn't explain enough, but Alard did a good job of filling us in on the details."

"Including how he threatened me?"

"Alard told us he threatened to put you in jail, which is where you'll end up anyhow."

"That is not true," Marrin protested. "That is not how he threatened me."

She tried to explain that Alard had blackmailed her, but George ignored her the rest of the way to the ranch. Marrin once caught a slight movement of his head in her direction, but by the time she turned, he was staring straight ahead again.

She tried to explain Alard's threats again, but stopped, too ashamed to give him the sordid details. It didn't matter. It was one small consolation that the truth was out, and at least Alard could no longer blackmail her.

They passed beneath the arched gate with the prominent circled M. "Ironic," George snorted. "God's mercy." He burned hostile eyes at her. "Something you won't be getting."

Marrin swallowed over a hard lump in her throat and braced her shoulders. She was about to enter the lion's den with Liam, George, and Alard all against her. She was a liar, a thief, a criminal, a sinner. She didn't dare ask anyone for mercy now. She didn't even know who she was anymore. She'd lost herself in her masquerade. George was right. She deserved no mercy. Not from Liam. Not from George. Not even from God. If there is a God.

A woman stood in the bank, clutching the poster long after the surrey disappeared. "I think we'd best show this to the sheriff," she said quietly.

No one disagreed.

CHAPTER 19:
Wanted

"She was not the one to weep that the sunshine had gone out of her life; she would make it shine again." —Mark Twain, *Tom Sawyer*

$\mathcal{L}$iam and Alard were waiting with Edith at the top of the front porch steps as George and Marrin arrived in the surrey. The tension was clear and painful, while Edith stood with pursed lips, worry wrinkles lining her forehead as she wrung her hands.

Marrin tried to take slower breaths to keep from feeling faint. She balled her fists, not from anger—there was none of that left in her—but to ease the weight of knowing she deserved their scorn and distrust. Nothing could excuse what she'd done. However, she wasn't exactly sure if she was more sorry for her sin or simply sorry she'd gotten caught.

She stopped at the foot of the steps, the rest of the group towering above her on the porch. They looked down, making her feel humbled and small, as though she were on trial—which she essentially was.

Facing them, she clasped her hands tightly at her waist to keep them from noticeably trembling. Her mouth was so dry, she could barely swallow. If only Alard weren't there. She managed to ignore his toothy snarl, rotating her body to keep him on the periphery of her vision.

Liam brandished her confession letter and cleared his throat. "So, you are Marrin Fournier of Amiens, France."

It was no use explaining or making up excuses. "Oui, monsieur," she said weakly before making up her mind to speak up boldly and more clearly: "Oui, monsieur. My real name is Marrin Fournier." She wouldn't allow herself to be timid now. She was here to tell everyone the truth.

"Explain yourself," Liam said sternly.

She stood at the foot of the porch steps, rocking from one foot to the other as she told much of her tale, omitting parts she didn't want Alard to hear. She also left out his repulsive blackmail threats. She articulated plainly and without emotion, making no attempt to garner sympathy as she answered their many questions.

"So, all this time you were just running a con—taking our food, our home, our help, your education—and laughing behind our backs?" George's question was an ice-cold statement.

His harsh words were a knife twisting in her guts. "That's true," she admitted.

"You lied to all of us," said Liam, his intonation more weary and sad than angry.

"Yes, I did." She dropped her head and stared at her feet, unconsciously kicking pieces of gravel. "I would tell you again how sorry I am, but sorry cannot make up for how I have hurt you all."

"You lied to my uncle for financial profit," said Alard, repugnance spewing from his mouth. "You realize it's a crime of fraud punishable by prison, hanging, or both."

You're the one who should go to prison or hang, she thought, longing to tell Liam about the wanted poster she'd seen in town, yet knowing he wouldn't believe her.

"There's no need to be so graphic and frighten the girl," said Liam sternly. "The crime she committed was against me alone, and I have the right to turn her in to the sheriff or send her back to Virginia, where she can work to pay off her indenture."

Marrin sucked her lower lip between her teeth. Suddenly, there was nothing she wanted more than to pay her debt to the people in Virginia. It was no more than she deserved. If Liam Stinson was merciful enough to keep her crimes a secret from the sheriff, she'd welcome a few years of service. It might save her sister, too, since there was a chance Robinette had been sent to work there in her place. *How wretched and selfish I've been to these kind people and to my own sister*, she grieved.

"She shouldn't stay another night in your home, Uncle," said Alard. "She should be in jail while you decide what…"

Alard's words trailed off as each person on the porch looked out over and behind Marrin's head and beyond. She twisted round to see a herd of horses approaching from the west, galloping in front of a trail of dust. They'd all seen the herd of wild horses before. Why would they be so interested in them now?

"Who do you think it is?" asked George.

Who? Marrin wondered, perplexed.

"It looks almost like a sheriff's posse," said Edith.

Marrin stiffened and jerked her head to George, who looked at her with wide eyes. "Are they coming for me?" Marrin asked.

"No, no," said Liam. "I've told no one about you."

George parted his mouth, his glance darting to Alard. Marrin gasped while a hand flew to cover her mouth.

"What have you done?" Alard snarled at Marrin as he charged down the porch steps, lunging to her side and pulling a pistol from his holster. George took a step toward them, but Alard pointed his gun back at him. "Stop right there," Alard demanded. Marrin felt the cold steel of the gun against the side of her head. "You want justice? You want to see this girl punished for what she's done? Then don't follow me."

He shoved Marrin down the steps and walked backward with her to where his horse was tethered to a hitching post.

"What's going on?" asked Liam. "What are you doing, Alard?"

"Seems this little shrew might have told our local sheriff the same crazy stupid lies she wrote about me in that letter to Carina," said Alard, tossing Marrin like a sack of grain over the back of the horse and swinging up behind her, painfully shoving her hips into the saddle horn. He fired his gun into the air, and Marrin's heart jumped into her throat. Surprisingly, she was still alive.

She heard shouts behind her and tried to push herself up to see, but was stuck head down, lying on her stomach, draped over the horse, and unable to see anything but the ground that began to speed beneath them as Alard galloped over the green pasture grass of Liam's grazing land.

The horse increased its speed, sending skull-pounding, teeth-crashing jolts through Marrin's body with each impact. She struggled again, craning her neck sideways to look backward beyond Alard's shin. Her abdomen throbbed with every galloping stride. One rider was gaining on them, with several other riders following close behind. Alard twisted in the saddle and fired his pistol over Marrin's head.

Please, God, don't let him shoot anyone! Marrin prayed, her ears still ringing from the clamor of the shot. She pressed her hands against the pulsing muscles of the horse's shoulder and tried to twist her body to look up at Alard, but she couldn't move through the thudding, galloping jolts. But something protruded from the top of Alard's stirruped boot right at the level of her nose— something brassy and shiny. A knife handle. She reached, grabbed at the air, and lurched. Pausing to catch her breath, she swayed with the pounding rhythm of the gallop and tried again, this time grasping the handle between bursts of swaying movement and finally pulling the blade from the boot. She stared at the weapon held tightly in her clammy palm.

Another loud pistol shot cracked above her head. She startled, cringed, and nearly dropped the knife. Glancing backward again, she watched the lone rider drawing steadily closer. Who was it? The sheriff? One of his deputies? It was hard to focus when everything was upside-down. And then she saw. It looked like… George? No, it couldn't be. He wouldn't put himself in harm's way, dodging Alard's bullets. He didn't care for her.

Alard fired again, but the pursuing riders kept their distance, pistols lowered. None dared risk shooting toward Alard as long as she was his hostage. Marrin was left with no choice but to act.

Bang! Alard fired once more. She panicked and made a desperate decision. She jabbed the knife into Alard's thigh, leaving it there as she hefted herself backward, feet down over the opposite side. A savage howl tore from Alard's lungs as she slid and shoved herself off the horse. The toes of her boots caught and bumped across the ground before her body hit the earth with a wrenching thud that mangled her ankle and scraped grit and gravel across her face. She came to a jarring halt on a tuft of grass.

All at once, a volley of pistol shots rang out nearby and sharply faded as the sky and sun and clouds tipped and spun. Marrin barely opened one eye, dizzy, head throbbing, crusts of salt and sweat stinging her wounded face. She tried to rise, but pain shot through her leg. Pushing herself onto her elbows, she crawled blindly.

"Marrin?" The deep, gruff shout of a man's voice floated to her ears. "Ca va, Marrin?" It sounded like George, but she wasn't sure until she saw him spring from his horse and run to her side amidst a torrent of hooves and dust rumbling past. Faint, yelping screams continued from Alard.

Marrin turned her throbbing head slightly. Through the blur of dust and grass, she heard a volley of gunfire and watched Alard slump and fall from his horse, his body flopping to the ground like a scarecrow nearly trampled by the other horses. Through blurred vision, she watched him struggle to raise himself to a kneeling position, scratching his nails in the dust. He tightened his fists around chunks of gravel, cursing and spitting. Drool hung in muddy threads from his lips.

Marrin barely had time to register what she'd witnessed before her limp, weak body was suddenly elevated from the ground. She recognized the spicy fragrance of soap and cinnamon and rested her head on George's chest.

Lifting her onto the saddle of his horse, George barked an order for her to hold on. He swung up behind, holding her tightly, pulling her body against his, securing an arm around her waist. Every small breath shot fire through her chest. She moaned, trying not to whimper. Her body slumped forward. Gray dust blurred, sounds muffled, and dizziness enveloped her. And the world went dark.

CHAPTER 20:
Sans Merci

"The quality of mercy . . . is twice blessed; It blesseth him that gives and him that takes…" Mark Twain, *The Prince and the Pauper*

Marrin was only slightly aware of being carried into the house and up the stairs to her room. Grim-faced, tight-lipped, and never looking her in the eye, George settled her on the bed and covered her with a light quilt. She barely heard Edith stomp up the steps and into the room to fuss over her, unlacing and removing her boots, washing her face, and shooing George away for not making himself more useful.

He left. And he did not return—not that day, not the next.

"Proud, unforgiving men, both of them," said Edith, shaking her head and smoothing Marrin's brow with tender fingers. "There, there, poor dear. Liam sent for the doctor. Just rest now. Rest will ease…."

Sleep or unconsciousness enveloped her, diminishing her pain. Somewhat.

During the fog of Marrin's convalescence, she vaguely remembered the doctor examining her and stating in hushed tones that she had broken ribs, a sprained ankle, and numerous cuts and bruises. It would take her weeks to recover.

In one of her blurred, confused waking spells, she knew Liam Stinson paid her a brief visit. He asked Edith how Marrin was doing before stiffly stating without emotion that he would allow her to recover enough to walk before deciding what to do with her.

As soon as he exited the room, Edith protested quietly to Marrin, unsure if she was listening: "How dare he?" The whispered words grated from her throat. "*Circle M*, the symbol of Greenwind Ranch, my foot. He's forgotten what mercy means."

"What is mercy?" Marrin breathed weakly, the vibration of her vocal cords weak in her chest.

"Oh, my dear," Edith exclaimed, "you're speaking at last! But don't try to talk. It will hurt too much." She walked to the desk and opened the French-English dictionary. "You asked what mercy is? Mercy is *miséricorde*."

"Oh, yes," rasped Marrin. "I do not want that. I deserve jail." She no longer cared that she might even have to share a cell with Alard. *Let them hang me or lock me away*, she thought. *There was nothing left of herself to save.* Hope had drained from her soul.

"You absolutely do *not* deserve jail," Edith protested. "I don't blame you a bit for all you did. If I were you, I could only hope to have enough courage to do the same. In fact, even your Aunt—Oh, I mean, Penelope. Of course, she wasn't your aunt. Anyhow, Penelope was very much like you. She would have done the same." Pain ripped through Marrin's chest as she shifted her weight in the bed. Suddenly, concentrating on Edith's words became too difficult, and sleep began to grab her again.

"I saw how Liam and George cared for you before all this," the housekeeper, cook, and friend went on, her motherly voice fading until she mentioned George's name. There was the glint of a tear in Edith's eye. "Yes, that's right. Even George. Don't think I haven't noticed the way he looks at you." Edith's hand compassionately stroked Marrin's hair. "It was by the grace of God that you survived such a dreadful fall from a speeding horse. You're lucky you didn't land on any rocks. I know God saved you…." Marrin didn't want to hear about God. If He existed, He wasn't someone she wanted to know. She heard nothing more as the weight of drowsiness caught and pulled her under once more.

Nearly a week passed before Marrin could stand on her own. Neither Liam nor George paid her another visit. Her only visitor was Edith, who every day proved a sweeter friend. The woman told her everything that was happening at the ranch, at the church, in town, and at the school, which was now closed for the summer. All the while, Marrin remained silent because it hurt too much to talk. And she had nothing to say except sorry. But neither George nor Liam was there to hear her apologies.

It was a bright, sultry Saturday morning when Marrin finally hobbled a few cringing steps across her bedroom floor, still desperately and fearfully avoiding coughs, sneezes, and deep breaths, all of which sent sharp, crackling fire through her broken and bruised ribcage. She settled into the desk chair and heard voices in the front yard. Raising herself, she parted the curtains and looked down to see her friends from school. They handed Edith a basket and drove away in a wagon. Very sweet. Very undeserved.

"From Milly and Colette," Edith told her as she set the basket on the desk. "So kind of them." She touched Marrin lightly on the shoulder. "Go ahead. See what they've brought you." Marrin took a painful, shallow breath and slowly lifted her arm, reaching to remove the handkerchief covering the contents of the basket. She winced as even the effort of lifting her arm shot spasms through her ribs, but she bit her lip and kept silent. Inside the basket were a jar of strawberry jam, freshly baked rolls, a small bouquet of wildflowers, and an envelope with the name *Carina* written in cursive. They must not know her real name yet.

Marrin opened the letter and read about the boys the two friends liked, their plans for the summer, how they missed her, and how much they wanted her to spend time with them in various upcoming activities–swimming, canoeing on local lakes, and joining them in a sewing circle. They even offered to keep teaching her English, so she'd be better prepared for the next school term.

"They are kind," Marrin said breathily, sniffing lightly.

"There, there," said Edith. "Are you crying? Don't cry, Marrin dear. You'll see your friends again soon."

"No, I won't, Edith," said Marrin. "If I'm not jailed or hanged, I'll be sent back east—to be an indentured servant."

"Utter nonsense," Edith barked, "I will not permit—"

"Edith, please," said Marrin blandly, "I don't care anymore. I sinned, and I will pay for it. I don't mind."

Edith knelt on the floor, so her eyes were level with Marrin's. "Marrin, you did wrong, and you confessed," she said sternly. "God forgives you, and so do I, so stop with your guilt this blessed minute and forgive yourself. It doesn't matter that certain others in this house haven't got the sense to offer you any mercy, but they will someday. I'm sure of it. Fact is, you also need to start forgiving those two stubborn mules for not forgiving you. Keep forgiving until the emotional pain goes away. It will get easier with practice, I promise. I know from personal experience. Forgiveness is a command from the Good Book itself, so you'd better do what it says. You hear me?"

"What Good Book?"

"The Bible, of course," Edith explained.

"Oh." Marrin's lips dragged downward. "I'm not sure I believe in God anymore," she said meekly.

Edith's eyes widened; then softened. "That's fine. He believes in you, and that's what matters." She pulled up a chair opposite Marrin. "Why don't you believe in God, sweetheart?" Edith asked.

"Could God really forgive me?"

"You bet your britches," she answered with a smile.

Marrin shook her head and winced. "What does that mean, Edith?"

"Oh!" Edith chuckled. "What I mean is yes, God can and will absolutely forgive you—if you're truly sorry and you tell Him so."

"I am sorry," she sniffed, "but I cannot forgive myself."

Edith shook her finger in Marrin's face. "You will forgive yourself, whether you feel like it or not. And that's an order, Marrin Fournier—not from me, but from God Himself. He knows what's best for you."

Marrin sighed, turned slowly, and looked out the window at rolling green hills and mountains in the distance.

"Confess your sins to God, ask His forgiveness, forgive others, and forgive yourself." Edith stood to her feet with a huff and a grunt. "Now you'd better lie down and rest again. You've tired yourself. I'll go get you a fresh pitcher of water and some chipped ice from the ice box."

Edith tucked her patient into bed again, and as soon as she left the room, Marrin reluctantly did as Edith had instructed.

"God, just in case You are real," she prayed, "I've decided to confess all my sins to You. Please forgive me.

And I forgive everyone—Liam, George, my aunt and uncle in Amiens, and even Alard. And please help me to forgive myself for all the bad things I've done. I'm sorry for them all."

She breathed heavily and relaxed as a strange blanket of peace and contentment fell upon her. When Edith returned, Marrin gave her a relaxed smile. "Maybe God is real," she said. "And I think He does forgive me."

Edith's eyes sparkled with tears. "I can see that. Watch and see how God is now free to work miracles in your life."

"Miracles?"

"Divine, supernatural acts of God."

"*Oui. Des miracles.*" Marrin let her eyelids flutter shut. "I do not deserve them, but they would be nice."

CHAPTER 21:
Rewards

"The two most important days in your life are the day you are born and the day you find out why." – Generally Attributed to Mark Twain

*T*he next day was Sunday, and Marrin was alone in the house. Edith had driven over in her wagon before church to fill a tub with hot water for her recovering patient, tenderly washing Marrin's hair before leaving for church with Liam and George.

After a healing soak, Marrin stiffly and gingerly stepped out of the tub and began dressing her bruised, aching body. Though her foundation garment helped to ease the pain of her broken ribs, she needed Edith's help putting it on, so she resorted to wearing only pantalettes and a chemise beneath a light calico dress.

Finally, clean and fresh, Marrin cringed as she struggled to twirl her wet hair into a loose bun on the back of her head, surprised at how being clean significantly improved her entire well-being. The gloom of her regrets and remorse lifted somewhat, and she almost believed she could forgive herself for at least some of the wrongs she'd done. Almost.

She wiggled her toes into a soft pair of slippers and limped from the bathroom, pausing at the top of the landing, where she braced herself for a slow descent. Though not devoid of grunts and groans, she made it to the parlor and eased herself into a soft chair to rest from her exertion, closing her eyes for a few minutes. Just a few minutes.

A loud rapping on the front door startled her from what had turned into a brief nap and Marrin placed an unsteady hand on her heart. Alone in the house, she wondered if she should answer the door. It might not be safe. The knocking clamored again.

"Miss Carina or Marrin or whatever your name is," a man's baritone voice shouted. "It's the sheriff. Are you home?"

Her heart crammed painfully up into her throat. Her first instinct was to hide and remain silent. But she stood on shaky legs. So today was the day. She was finally well enough. She was going to jail. "I'm coming," she called, her voice barely audible as she shuffled slowly to the front door.

"I won't come in, since you're probably unaccompanied, but I'm leaving an envelope out here for you," said the sheriff.

"What?" Marrin halted as she reached the foyer, confused. "But I am going to jail."

"Why would you do that?" the sheriff asked.

"Because I am…a criminal," she spoke haltingly.

There was a pause. "I think maybe you need a translator who speaks French, ma'am," he said with a chortle. "It sounded like you said you're a criminal. I know that's not what you meant."

"But I *am* a criminal, and I need to go to jail," she repeated.

Another pause. "Ma'am, you're clearly still unwell after your terrible fall from that horse and getting all those injuries. You're not talking sense. I'll just leave this envelope here for you and be on my way. You get well now, you hear?"

"But I am coming with you," she said through the closed door.

"No, no, no, you're definitely not doing that," the sheriff commanded firmly. She heard his footsteps retreating down the porch stairs. "Mr. Stinson will be back from church shortly." He added in a lower voice that Marrin barely heard, "He'd better get back soon, 'cause you're plumb delirious."

Marrin stepped outside and watched the sheriff heave onto his horse. "Oh, hey there!" he called, seeing her in the doorway. He gestured to the porch. "I left the reward money there for you, ma'am! I contacted the banks and railroads, and they sent over your bounty money for catching that wanted criminal, Alard Lejeune. Thank you for your help. Good day, ma'am." He gave her a quick wave and rode away.

Reward money? A brown paper envelope lay at her feet. Bending in a stiff, painful squat, she picked up the parcel and carried it inside. Glancing at the clock in the parlor, she knew that George, Liam, and Edith would be home any minute, so she began her arduous journey up the stairs, stopping every two steps to rest and wipe perspiration from her brow.

Why had Liam apparently not reported her crimes to the sheriff? Was he waiting until she was well to do so? Or maybe he was planning to send her back to Virginia instead of jail. Yes, that must be it.

She reached her room, closed the door, lowered herself onto the desk chair, and gulped a glass of water. Opening the sheriff's envelope, she peeked inside. At that moment, Liam's surrey announced its return to Greenwind. She pulled crisp bills from the envelope and counted one hundred dollars. One hundred dollars! She could put that with the money she'd taken from Alard and try to escape again—although she felt some guilt knowing Alard had stolen the money she'd stolen from him.

Reaching into the envelope again, she withdrew a letter expressing gratitude on behalf of several bankers and railroad tycoons. It was signed by a United States Marshall. It also explained that the outlaw Alard Lejeune had been shipped to the State of Colorado for a court hearing, where he would be sentenced, and probably hanged for theft, kidnapping, and murder. She let the letter fall to the floor.

Murder? Marrin hadn't known that—hadn't wanted to know.

Death by hanging? Suddenly, she felt that not even Alard deserved such an end before he had time to confess his sins and ask God for forgiveness. What would Carina think of losing her brother that way? What would Liam think of losing his nephew? She covered her eyes with her hands and wept, praying for Alard's soul, trying hard to control the sobs that convulsed her aching ribs.

Edith arrived, and Marrin told her about the sheriff's visit. "Please, Edith," said Marrin, "could you ask Liam to come here and talk to me?"

Liam meekly and respectfully entered the room, inquiring as to how she felt and, with genuine concern in his voice, asking why she'd been crying.

"Why did you not tell the sheriff about my crimes, Mr. Stinson?" Marrin questioned, reverting to her native language as she wrapped her arms tightly about her chest to ease the pain. Liam gave her a blank, quizzical look. "The sheriff came today and gave me an envelope," she continued. "I thought he came to take me to jail, but he did not. He gave me a letter and reward money for telling him about Alard." She handed Liam the money, but he refused to take it. He stood and stepped backward, nearly bumping into Edith.

"I want you to take it, Mr. Stinson. And here is the letter from a United States Marshall stating that Alard is to be tried and may be hung for his crimes. I am so sorry, for he is your nephew." She struggled to fight more tears as Liam took the letter, but still wouldn't touch the money. "Is there any hope for his soul, Uncle—I mean, Mr. Stinson? Is there any way to delay his hanging to give him time to confess his sins and ask God for mercy?"

There was a long, uncomfortable pause while a flash of imperceptible emotions crossed Liam's face.

"Please read the letter, Liam," Edith urged.

He complied and, when he had finished, set it on the desktop. "I have to think," he said gruffly.

"Yes, indeed," grunted Edith from where she stood watching and listening near the door. "You'd better."

He turned and strode from the room. "I'm glad you're feeling better," he added, casting the words over his shoulder as he made his departure.

If Liam wouldn't turn her in, she'd turn herself in. "I'll take the money, buy a ticket east, and find my indentured family in Virginia," Marrin murmured.

"You'll do no such thing," Edith interjected. She snatched the reward money from Marrin's hand and stashed it into an apron pocket. "I'll hold onto this until you're well enough to think rationally."

Marrin pouted. She still had the money she'd stolen from Alard. She'd buy her train ticket with that and head east as soon as possible.

Another stiflingly hot summer week passed, and still, the sheriff didn't come to take her to jail. Nor did Liam speak to her. George didn't either. In fact, they averted their gaze whenever she limped past them in the hallway, on the stairs, or on the wraparound porch. Oddly, however, though the lack of communication thickened the atmosphere, Marrin felt neither sorrow nor anger toward them. She didn't even feel self-pity at their treatment of her. She felt true forgiveness. And it felt good.

As her strength returned, her pain lessened, and she ventured farther outdoors for short strolls, using a walking stick that Liam made for her. Sometimes she would carry her carpetbags to strengthen her arms—in preparation for her long walk to the train station.

On her daily laps around the house, Marrin paid regular visits to the barn, spending time with Pinto and Liam's dog, Jacques. They were good listeners, and she shared her heart with them. As she nuzzled her face against Pinto's soft nose or sat on a bale of hay, stroking Jacques' wiry fur, she found God in that barn too, sensing His peace, presence, and comfort.

"Dear Lord, I'm no longer afraid to go wherever my punishment takes me," she prayed in her native tongue. "I used to feel so lonely. But I am no longer alone with You in my life now."

It's where she finally surrendered everything to the Lord and decided to fully forgive herself too. And she came to realize that a lack of grace for herself was actually quite selfish and did nothing to bless the people she loved.

It was very early one July morning when Marrin slipped from the house before dawn, knowing she'd make the three-and-a-half miles to Yreka in plenty of time to catch the noon train. Walking slowly and taking plenty of pauses to rest, she reached the depot in a little over two hours.

The sun peeped over the horizon, casting a pink glow on the whispery clouds. Marrin collapsed onto a bench and leaned heavily on the wall behind her. It was six o'clock, and she had two hours to wait until the ticket office opened. Then it would be four more hours until she boarded the train—too much time to sit on that hard, uncomfortable wooden bench.

Rising, she peered up Miner Street to the already bustling town and made her way to a corner café that was open for breakfast. Seated at a lonely, shadowed corner table, she ate a light meal and drank a glass of milk. Fatigued from her walk, she placed her carpetbag on top of the cleared table. Settling her head on the soft fabric, she meant only to rest her eyes for a moment…

The café filled and emptied several times as Marrin slept, undisturbed.

"Carina?" Marrin lifted her head and blinked, rubbing her eyes and staring into Collette's worried face. "Carina, is that you? What are you doing here?"

"What time is it?" Marrin asked, panic-stricken.

"A little after one o'clock. I finished taking care of my baby sister and came here for a late lunch—"

"No, no, no!" Marrin cried. "How did I fall asleep?"

"What's wrong?" Collette asked.

"Oh, dear, I've missed my train," Marrin groaned. "Could I perhaps stay with you for the night and catch tomorrow's train?"

"I…I suppose so," Collette stammered. "But where are you going by train?"

"I have to leave. I am sorry, Collette. I will miss you, but bad things have happened, and I must leave."

Collette's eyes popped. "Did someone at the ranch hurt you?"

"No, of course, not. It was I who hurt everyone, and I need to leave to make their lives easier." Collette asked more questions, but Marrin refused to give any details.

"I suppose it would be all right for you to stay with us," Collette reluctantly agreed. Marrin gathered her things. "But

I came here to eat lunch. I'm starved." Marrin groaned and dropped her satchel to the floor. She'd eat another meal there with her friend but hoped to leave before anyone else recognized her. It was surprising that the café's owner had allowed her to sleep at the table all those hours. Now if she could just make it through the meal and avoid any more of Collette's questions…

CHAPTER 22:
Unexpected Visitors

"Get your facts first, then you can distort them as you please." Mark Twain

It was late in the afternoon when a stagecoach invaded the driveway and stopped in front of the porch of the big, pink Stinson house. George stopped in the middle of brushing and currying Pinto and stomped out of the barn to meet the unexpected arrivals.

"May I be of assistance?" he asked in a stiff tone.

A young woman's face peeked from the coach window, and George's jaw tightened. "Oh, Carina," he grumbled. "I mean Marrin. We wondered where you'd gone. What are you doing gallivanting about in a stagecoach without permission?" Marrin touched a gloved hand to her lips and stifled a laugh as she sat back and spoke to someone else in the carriage.

Typical of the lying, conniving little brat to disappear without a word and get into trouble with strangers, he thought. "Best get yourself back into the house," George barked.

The girl laughed outright. "Je vais entrer dans la maison," she said with a cheerful, tinkling voice as she hopped nimbly from the coach. "Où est Uncle Liam?"

"Probably inside," said George with a jerk of his head, "but you'd better stop calling him *Uncle*." He snorted. "I see you've miraculously recovered from your injuries. Not surprising. You probably faked how badly you were hurt. How you got the doctor to diagnose you with broken ribs, I'll never know." She ignored him, and he cast a suspicious eye to three other passengers alighting from the coach—a prim, middle-aged woman dressed in refined clothing, a dapper gentleman in a suit who gathered luggage from the vehicle before paying the driver. The third passenger was a young girl of about twelve or thirteen.

"Hey, now!" George exclaimed. "Who are you folks and what makes you think you can stay here?" The gentleman stepped to Marrin's side and whispered something into her ear in French. As he spoke, his lips touched Marrin's earlobe in a provocative manner.

"How dare you?!" shouted George, lunging at the man and punching him squarely on the jaw, sending him thudding with a heavy sprawl into the dust. "No need to be gettin' so familiar with Marrin, no matter how wicked she is," George commanded, shaking his fist at the man where he lay on the ground. He jabbed a finger in the man's face. "You can march your big city buttocks back to town and get yourself on the next train to wherever you came from." He spun back to Marrin to give her another scathing reprimand, but she ignored him, reaching to help the injured man from the ground as the stagecoach made a hasty retreat.

"Are you sure you're all right?" Marrin asked the man, still speaking French.

"Perfectly," he said, massaging his jaw. "Go on into the house now, Carina."

Marrin spun, raced up the porch steps, and disappeared into the house. The younger girl stood arms akimbo and shouted angrily at George for hitting the man, while the older well-dressed lady calmed the child and turned to George. "S'il vous plaît, monsieur, puis-je rencontrer Monsieur Liam Stinson?" she asked.

"Wait here," George ordered, detaining the three visitors with an outstretched palm. "Let me fetch Mr. Stinson."

The man, woman, and girl looked at one another with confused expressions as George bounded up the porch steps. He was about to place his hand on the front doorknob when Liam opened it. "There you are, Liam. I don't know who these people are or where they've come from. The brat Marrin came back with these total strangers who—"

Liam didn't appear to hear a word. Instead, he walked past George and stomped awkwardly down a few steps, staring at the fancy woman in the driveway. Stopping halfway, Liam's jaw dropped. "Gabrielle?" he asked.

George knotted his brows. Liam knew the woman? How? Who was she? And was he so familiar with her that he'd call her by her given name?

"Liam?" the woman responded.

"Gabrielle, I…I can't believe it's you." Liam was speaking French. He descended the stairs and approached the Frenchwoman, who placed her hands in his and gave him a quick peck on both cheeks.

"Liam," she repeated.

"Gabrielle," he said for the third time, her name easing from his lips.

"Oui, c'est moi," she replied.

Liam seemed to recover from his daze as he welcomed the guest. He introduced her as Mademoiselle Gabrielle Dumont.

Gabrielle Dumont? The woman in Europe that Liam loved a long time ago? Little was making sense to George. He followed them into the house and found Marrin in the parlor.

"You're not going to strike me, too?" Marrin asked teasingly, stepping back defensively as the face-punched gentleman pushed past him and sprang to her side. He took a protective stance between her and George as the twelve-year-old girl hurried to stand beside Gabrielle and hold her hand.

"Keep away from Carina," warned the man.

"Please don't hurt her," said the young girl.

"Of course, I won't hurt her," stammered George. "And her name's not Carina. She lied about that."

"I must say, I am unfamiliar with American customs," said Marrin, "but striking visitors and knocking them down in the dust does not seem a hospitable gesture in any culture."

"Stop the theatrics, Marrin Fournier," George growled.

"You still think I'm Marrin?" The girl's mouth curved in a wry half-smile. "I am Carina Lejeune. Clearly, you see the resemblance between Marrin and me." George pursed his lips, refusing to let the girl think he was gullible.

Marrin or Carina giggled and looked at the gentleman beside her. "And I suppose you thought my Anton was behaving inappropriately with your Marrin? She never told me about you. But that explains why you hit him." She touched the man's cheek. "Poor darling." Her attention darted about the room. "Where is Mademoiselle Marrin Fournier anyhow? I can't wait to see her."

"She's...she's...I don't know..." George stuttered, looking to Liam for help. Was this lady really Carina?

"What do you mean?" Marrin or Carina demanded.

"I don't think I've...seen...Mademoiselle Marrin today," Liam stuttered.

Edith stepped in from the kitchen at that moment, wiping her hands on her apron and gesturing toward the group in the parlor. "Have you gone mad, Liam? What do you mean you haven't seen Marrin? She's standing right here in this room."

Liam shook his head. "I…I don't think this is Marrin. I think this really is *Carina*. The *real* Carina. Look at her eyes, George."

George blinked, not processing at first. "Blue," he breathed. "This lady's eyes are blue."

"Exactly," Liam said, flinching and adjusting his cravat.

"What do you mean she's the *real* Carina?" asked Edith. "Marrin, what is going on here? Who are these people?"

"I am not Marrin or Marrin or whatever you call her. I am Carina Lejeune. I've come here from Belgium with my friends and my fiancé, Anton. Apparently, Marrin is gone." She leveled a stare into Liam's eyes. "Why are you not looking for her?"

"We were angry with her for deceiving us," said Liam, his tone limp.

"So angry that you let her run away?" Carina's eyes bulged. "Or did you kick her out?"

Liam and George looked at one another, their faces registering confusion and alarm.

"Oh, no!" Gabrielle exclaimed. "Please tell me you didn't cast her out, Liam!"

"Gabrielle, I…" Liam began.

"If you're Carina," said Edith, "then where's Marrin? I'm so confused—and frightened. Nobody tells me anything."

"Liam, we must find Marrin," said Gabrielle, drawing the shy young girl closer. "This is Robinette—her little sister.

Carina nodded sharply. "Marrin's sister from Amiens. Being with her again was Marrin's greatest hope."

Edith pressed a hand to her mouth. "She told me she meant to sell herself into indentured service in Virginia. She said she deserved it—for her sins."

Gabrielle's face drained of color. "Then she could be out there alone. Injured. Believing no one wanted her."

"If you're not Marrin, we must find her!" Edith exclaimed. "She told me she was going to sell herself into slavery in Virginia as an indentured servant. She said she deserved the punishment for her sins."

"The poor girl could be out there all alone on her own!" Gabrielle cried.

"Where's her room?" asked Carina. "Is anything missing? Did she pack her things before leaving?"

"I'll check," said Edith, dashing up the stairs.

"And look for a note," said George.

"Yes, if she left for good, maybe she left a note like she did before," said Liam.

Gabrielle glared at Liam. "She ran away *before*? Why?"

"It's a long story." Liam's countenance was sheepish.

"You act like you expected her to run away again! What did you do to her?" Gabrielle demanded.

"Nothing. I…I was angry with her," Liam sputtered.

"We both were," George admitted.

"You were angry because she pretended to be me?" asked Carina.

"Not exactly," said Liam. "Angry because she was dishonest. She lied to me. To all of us."

"But it was all *my* fault," Carina protested. "I'm the one who put her up to the whole charade. I lied and made her lie. I'm the one you should be angry with."

"Oh, Liam," whispered Gabrielle, worry and disappointment mingling in her expression.

"If she's run away, we must go and look for her. When did you last see her?"

"Last night," said George. Then, more quietly, "Not this morning."

"Carina's breath caught. "Then she could have left on the noon train."

Robinette swiped at her eyes. "I've come so far to see my sister again."

"She's gone," Edith called from the upstairs landing. "All her things are missing—but she left no note."

Gabrielle closed her eyes. "Was she even strong enough to walk into town alone?"

George hesitated. "She'd been regaining her strength. I saw it."

"From what?" Gabrielle demanded.

"Alard," Liam said.

Carina turned pale. "What did he do to her?"

"He kidnapped her," George said. "She escaped—but she was injured."

Robinette let out a small, broken sound. "My poor sister."

"What if Alard has kidnapped her again?" asked Carina.

"Impossible. He was captured by the sheriff and put in jail," said Liam.

"Jail?" asked Carina, blinking. "Where?"

"He's somewhere in Colorado awaiting trial," Liam explained.

"Trial?" Carina paled. "What will happen to him?"

Liam shook his head. "It's not good. There's no soft way to put this. He committed other serious crimes besides kidnapping, so he may be hanged."

Carina's mouth dropped as she collapsed into a chair. "He hurt Marrin? So badly she couldn't walk?" Anton knelt to comfort her while Edith hurried to fetch a glass of water.

George left the room, grabbing his hat from a peg on the wall on his way to the front door. He had driven her away once with his anger. He would not fail her again.

"Where are you going?" asked Liam.

"To look for Marrin," he said.

"Not by yourself, you're not," said Liam, bounding down the hallway to the door.

"We can ask around," said George. "If she's still in town, we'll find her."

"Wait for me!" Gabrielle cried.

"Ride with me, Gabrielle," said Liam. "We'll take my surrey. George, you ride ahead of us."

The door slammed, and they were gone, leaving the others to wait. And worry.

CHAPTER 23:
The Search

"Nothing can be more depressing than a sudden loss of faith." –Mark Twain, *Tom Sawyer*

The sun was low in the sky and tinging the clouds with color when Marrin Fournier stepped out the back door of the sweltering interior of her friend's house to encounter a boisterous breeze that blew wisps of tangled curls, sticking them to her sweat-damp face.

Sighing onto a slat-backed chair, she tucked her skirt between her legs and dropped her head to her hands. The door opened behind her. Marrin lifted her heavy head a few inches. Collette and her mother, Mrs. Marchand, joined her on the porch.

"Edith told me everything a week ago," said Mrs. Marchand. She spoke French.

"And Mother's just told me," added Collette. "What a wild and exciting story!"

Mrs. Marchand slid a couple of chairs in front of Marrin. "Collette, don't encourage her."

Marrin leaned back to face them, gripping her ribs in a hug.

Collette's mother inhaled and exhaled before venturing further. "Mademoiselle Marrin, I cannot let you stay here. Both Edith and Mr. Stinson are surely worried sick about you. They're probably out looking for you now. Think of that. The two of them wandering about, knocking on doors, calling for you until they're hoarse. I'm sure they have all their ranch hands out searching, too." Marrin wanted to protest, but Mrs. Marchand took her hands in hers. "I must insist on returning you to your uncle's ranch immediately."

"I think you're wrong, Madame Marchand. I don't think they'd search for me. They want me gone."

She held Marrin's hands in a firmer grip. "I refuse to believe that."

"Mr. Stinson has barely spoken to me since I told him the truth."

"Well, even if Mr. Stinson is angry with you, Edith is not, I assure you." Mrs. Marchand tipped Marrin's chin upward. "She's grown quite fond of you, in spite of everything." Marrin looked down and away. "You listen to me, mademoiselle. Collette's father and I will take you back to Greenwind Ranch." She stood, pulled her chair back into position, squared her shoulders, and slapped at her wind-whipped apron. "It's too hot to eat in the house, so we'll eat out here on the porch. After our meal, we'll be on our way."

"May I go too?" Collette was already arranging chairs around a circular table.

"Normally, I'd ask you to stay home to watch your brother and sister but under the circumstances, with Marrin being your friend, I will ask Madame Alarie if they can stay at her house this evening."

Collette beamed with gratitude as she hurried back inside to prepare supper with her mother, leaving Marrin to sit alone on the porch, knots of dread balling in her stomach. If only she hadn't missed the train.

She glanced at the door to the Marchand home. "I've caused so much trouble already," she whispered to herself. "If I must face Greenwind Ranch, I'll do it alone."

Hobbling stiffly down the porch steps, Marrin picked up her satchel and walked as quickly as she could across the yard and back toward the south end of town, where she turned and began her trek to the ranch. She'd already walked the distance earlier that morning; she could do it again. And hopefully save people the trouble of looking for her—if they ever really meant to search for her at all.

By the time George Royer turned his horse back toward Greenwind Ranch, night's shadows had begun to fall across the Shasta Valley. He'd spent a few hours asking around town for Marrin or Marrin, referring to her as Carina for clarity's sake. Finally, he found someone who'd seen her at the corner café with her friend Collette that afternoon. He stopped by the Marchand home and was relieved to hear them say Marrin was there, sitting on the back porch. But when they all went outside to see her, she was gone.

"Maybe she's headed back to the ranch," Collette suggested.

George's shoulders slumped. "I doubt that."

"I tried to convince her that you and Mr. Stinson were no longer angry with her," said Mrs. Marchand as her husband arrived home from work.

"And did she believe you?" George queried. Collette and her mother exchanged a worried glance. "Of course, not," he scoffed. "We gave her no reason to believe that."

Though they offered to join him in the search, George thanked them and decided to take their advice, heading back to Greenwind, riding away at a gallop and praying Marrin wasn't hiding out somewhere for the night, still determined to take the train back East. If he didn't find her back at the house, he'd ride out to town again and look for her again. Everywhere.

He rode past the school and onto the trail heading east—a trail filled with bittersweet memories of when Carina—or Marrin, rather—had first learned to ride a horse. His heart caught in his throat as he descended into the draw where Marrin had taken that tumble from Pinto one morning on the way to school. It seemed so long ago now. And he realized he wasn't angry with her anymore. He wasn't even hurt by her deceptions. He felt something completely new and different. He suddenly missed her and wanted her back more than anything. And all at once, his reasons for harboring anger toward Marrin felt dull and pointless.

He thought of the way her laughter lit up the dinner table—even when it wasn't appropriate. Of her poor etiquette, yet her stubborn determination to learn. Of her cute and clumsy ways. Of her quiet prayers in the barn, whispered to Pinto and Jacques when she thought no one was listening. Yes. That's when he knew.

He wanted to take her back to reunite with her sister, Robinette. Wanted to see the joy in her eyes. He wanted to know how she'd react to seeing Carina again. He wanted to hear both young ladies' adventurous stories. He wanted to forgive Marrin—as if she needed his forgiveness at all. He wanted only good things for her.

She could be out alone in the dark, rejected, feeling abandoned, and still bruised from her recent injuries. Although it was summertime, night temperatures dipped low and could cause hypothermia. He didn't want her to be alone and shivering in the cold. He…

His heart froze for a second as a lone figure appeared at the crest of the hill before him. It was the silhouette of a woman, limping along in the first rays of milky moonlight, carpetbag in hand as a breeze kicked up dust and tossed her unruly mass of curls that shone like melted chocolate dipped in starlight. Marrin. He'd been smitten with her from the moment they met.

Giving his horse's ribcage a squeeze, George galloped across a scatter of pebbles and up the rise, startling Marrin where she stopped and spun round to face him, dropping her bag on the ground and stumbling backward until she began to lose her balance. Springing from his horse, George leaped to her side, steadying her with an arm about her waist.

She unraveled herself from his clasp; then shoved her hands against his chest, avoiding the fervent look in his eyes. "I'm fine, I'm fine."

He grabbed her hands and held them tightly. "Marrin…Mademoiselle Marrin, I want to apologize to you."

"No, don't."

"I was wrong to be so angry with you."

"You were not wrong." She wriggled against him. "You had every right to be angry." He let go, and she pulled her hands from his grasp. "I lied to you and everyone, and *I* am the one who is sorry, Monsieur Royer." The symphony of crickets and frogs grew louder as she picked up her satchel and increased her wobbly pace toward Greenwind Ranch.

George removed his hat and ran a hand through his hair. She looked small and pitiful. How much pain was she in after walking to town, and now most of the way back to the ranch? "Are you coming back home?" George wanted to know.

"It's not my home," said Marrin. "I'm going back to tell Mr. Stinson that I'm all right before I leave. I don't want anyone wasting their time looking for me."

"Where will you go?" George grabbed his horse's lead rope and trotted behind her.

"Jail or to work as an indentured servant back East," she said gruffly.

"Please wait. Liam doesn't want that, and neither do I."

"Ha," she laughed bitterly. "Mr. Stinson made it very clear he wants me gone. And I know you do too."

"That's not true." He cleared a knot of gravel in his throat. "Well, actually, it is true that we *were* angry, and we wanted you gone for a short time—at first," he admitted, "but neither of us feels that way anymore. We were hurt, is all. We've been worried about you. Liam finally realized something was wrong, and most of Liam's ranch hands are out searching for you now."

"I must leave. I don't deserve any mercy—not from anyone."

"You can't do that. Not now that…" It wasn't his place to say anything to Marrin about Carina and Robinette. He wanted her to find out about them herself.

"Now that what?" she asked tentatively, skimming precariously on a scatter of loose stones near the bottom of the hill. George reached out to steady her elbow, but she yanked it away with a wince. "I'm fine."

They walked a few paces, so close he was tempted to touch her hair.

"Now that what?" she asked again.

"Now that…we realized how much we missed you when you were gone." She ignored him. "I understand why you and Carina agreed to your scheme. I also understand my feelings for you." Her pace didn't slow. Was she listening? "I'm in love with you, Marrin." That stopped her.

She turned to face him, and the moonlight sparkled in her eyes. "Why would you tell me such a lie?"

"I'm not lying." He took a step closer, and she shook her head.

"I don't believe you." She spun away again. "And I don't care. I'm leaving tomorrow."

George's heart lurched with grief. "But you'll see that we do care for you, and you didn't deserve the way we treated you. I rejected you, ignored you, shunned you. I tried to make you feel guilty when I knew you already felt ashamed."

"I don't harbor any ill will toward you or anyone," she sighed. "Just let me be." He slowed his pace as she walked ahead of him, the volume of crickets and frogs still singing in the dark.

"Marrin, no. I can't leave you." There was no hint of a response. "Did you hear me? I said I love you, Marrin!" he shouted, his voice echoing in the dark. A faint sob broke from her throat, and he ran to her, placing his hands on her shoulders and turning her to him. He took the bag from her grasp and tossed it to the ground. "Please, Marrin," he whispered, "forgive me for all the ways I've hurt you. I was wrong."

"I can't forgive you." Her barely audible reply came from lips that were mere inches from his. They tempted him almost beyond reason, but he knew that to kiss her might cause her more suffering.

The cold, heavy remorse in his chest was almost too much to bear. "I understand if you can't forgive me," he said, the words like sawdust in his mouth.

"I can't forgive you because there's nothing to forgive," Marrin said. The tears on her cheeks glistened. "I deserve hatred and anger from you for what I've done, and it's all right if you feel that way."

"But I don't hate you. I can't hate you. I forgive you for everything. You did what you had to do to save your life. I would have done the same. Anyone would. Well, anyone remarkably brave, that is." She hung her head and bit her lip, making him tremble with an aching desire to press his lips to hers. "Please believe me. I want to care for you, Marrin, as no one has ever cared for you before."

She backed away from him. "No, that's too much."

"Maybe too much for you to hear right now, but in time maybe…?" His words were thick and tight with emotion. "I want to show you that I care. That I truly love you."

"Please," she sighed, "just walk me home. I'm tired and confused. I can't think anymore."

He said nothing more after that. Picking up her satchel, he strapped it onto the saddlebag and hauled himself into the saddle. He reached down, offering his hand. She acquiesced, and she pulled her up to sit behind him, wrapping her thin arms around his waist.

He regretted that he'd said too much. He'd scared her with too much emotion, practically begging her to love him back. That wasn't fair to her. He wouldn't doubt it if she ran away from him for good now. But what was done was done, and she was right. It was late, and she was exhausted.

The house was mostly dark when they arrived back at Greenwind. George lifted Marrin from the saddle and walked her into the house, carrying her bag. They were met by Liam, who was waiting up for them in the parlor. He crossed the floor to Marrin and folded her into his arms. Bending, he kissed the top of her head.

"Thank the Lord you've come home, Marrin," said Liam. "I'm sorry for treating you so badly. Please, please forgive me, child." He released her and held her at arm's length; then he pointed to a photograph of Greenwind Ranch's gate with the grand Victorian mansion in the background. "Did I ever tell you what Greenwind's *Circle M* brand stands for?"

"No, actually, but…" She decided to let Liam explain.

"It's a constant reminder to me of God's eternal, unending mercy," Liam said. "Something I let myself forget. And something I must extend to you as I hope you'll extend to me."

"Of course," Marrin whispered, her cheeks damp with fresh tears. "But can you please forgive me?"

Mr. Stinson tucked a wayward curl behind her ear and glanced up to the ceiling. "Thank You, Jesus," he said. "Of course I forgive you." He sucked in a deep breath and addressed both George and Marrin. "It has been a long day.

I'll write a note and leave it on the door, telling searchers that you've come home safely. Let's all get some sleep, and we'll have a good talk in the morning. Understood?"

"Yes, sir," they both said in unison.

George swallowed over a rock in his throat and said good night to Marrin. She refused to acknowledge him.

"How much did you tell her?" Liam asked in a hush.

"Nothing," said George.

"Good. She can rest tonight and find out everything in the morning."

"Just make sure she doesn't escape again," said George.

"We'll keep watch," Liam promised. "Thank you for bringing her home." He eyed George head-on. "Have you told her how you feel about her?"

George's shoulders rose and fell. "I told her, but I don't think she feels the same way about me."

"Give her time," said Liam. "She needs to learn to trust you again—to trust both of us."

CHAPTER 24:
Revelations

"We can secure other people's approval if we do right and try hard, but our own is worth a hundred of it, and no way has been found out of securing that." - Mark Twain, *Following the Equator, Pudd'nhead Wilson's New Calendar*

Marrin rose, washed, and dressed gingerly, still avoiding too much movement in her ribs and shoulders. She was about to step out her bedroom door when she stopped and listened. Voices downstairs were speaking French. Who could they be? Collette and her family, perhaps? She tiptoed to the balcony and peeked over to see her own reflection staring up at her! She took a few cautious steps down the staircase.

"Marrin!" Carina leaped to her and hugged her tightly, causing her to emit a brief yelp. "Oh, I'm so sorry! I forgot about your accident!" She let go and dragged Marrin to the foot of the stairs to stand in the parlor, which was filled with guests. "Look, Marrin! Look who we brought for you!"

Marrin blinked in stupefied surprise at a chair across the room, where sat a young girl with rosy cheeks and wide, watery eyes.

The girl stood. "Bonjour, Marrin," she said softly.

The wind was knocked out of Marrin as she gasped. "Robinette? Is it really you?" She ran to her sister and held her while both of them wept with joy. "Oh, my sweet little Robin." Marrin cupped the little face in her hands and wiped the tears. Turning to Carina, she mouthed the words, *Thank you.*

She flicked her eyes about the room. Liam was there with a finely dressed woman, whom she recognized—her aunt, who used to visit her when Marrin was a child. Mademoiselle Gabrielle. Carina was there with a man she assumed was her fiancé. George and Edith were absent.

"I received your letter, Marrin," Carina said, watching Marrin with a proud smile. "You asked me to deliver your letter to Robinette. I couldn't go to Amiens by myself—we look too much alike—but I asked Gabrielle to help."

"Aunt Gabrielle Dumont," whispered Marrin, casting her eyes to the elegant woman, who approached and kissed Marrin on both cheeks.

"I knew Carina couldn't go there looking so much like you, Marrin," Gabrielle explained. "I know your aunt and uncle. Do you remember me?" Marrin nodded. "I used to visit you and your mother from time to time." She shot a look at Liam. "Should I tell her?"

Mr. Stinson stepped forward to face Carina and Marrin. "I've discovered the most shocking truth. Gabrielle will tell you, but you must both sit. Please."

They sat side by side on the settee, clasping hands, while the graceful, stylish Gabrielle settled on a footstool before them. "My dears, you are *my* daughters—both of you. And Mr. Stinson is your father."

Gasps sucked air from the room. Carina's fiancé squirmed uncomfortably. Marrin's jaw dropped.

"It's true," said Liam, hanging his head. "Mademoiselle Dumont and I spent some time together many years ago when I left Belgium to visit France."

"We started courting, and my parents did not approve,"

Gabrielle interrupted. "They forced me into an engagement with another man."

"I emigrated to America and settled in California, brokenhearted," Liam explained.

Gabrielle continued: "When my parents discovered I was with child out of wedlock, they sent me away to Switzerland to wait out my pregnancy and give birth…to you two—nearly identical twin daughters." Marrin and Carina stared at one another. "My engagement was broken, and I remained a spinster for the rest of my life. One of you was sent to live with a dear friend of mine." She peered deeply into Marrin's eyes. "Your mother was my closest friend. Her name was Marrin. I named you after her. She and her husband adopted you. And did you ever know that your adopted mother came from a wealthy family?" She sighed. "Unfortunately, her parents disowned her when she married your father for love."

Marrin snapped her open mouth shut again and swallowed. All of this was overwhelming and difficult to comprehend.

She turned to Carina. "And you, Carina, were sent to live with Liam's sister and husband in Antwerp. We all promised never to tell Liam the truth."

Back to Marrin. "I visited you often when you were very young. Your mother called me 'Aunt Gabrielle.' When your adopted parents died, Marrin, you and your sister Robinette were sent to live with Robinette's aunt and uncle, your mother's brother and his wife. I would try to visit on occasion, but your aunt seldom let me see you." A tear welled and slid down her cheek. "I saw that they favored Robinette over you, my poor dear, and I'm so sorry. Robinette was their own flesh and blood niece, but Marrin, you were not."

"And you, Carina," she said, leveling her gaze at her daughter. "Liam's sister and her husband did adopt you, but I was devastated when they sent you away to boarding school, where I was not allowed to visit."

"So, Alard and I are cousins, not brother and sister," Carina breathed.

Gabrielle nodded.

"Neither Gabrielle nor your mother, Carina," Liam interjected, "ever told me a thing." His tone was bitter.

"Because we had an agreement, Liam," Gabrielle protested softly. "I wanted to tell you everything. I wanted to keep my babies. But they were taken from me."

Liam's countenance was shadowed. "So many people were taken from me." He shook his head and scrubbed his face with his hands. "I have so many reasons to be angry. But I have many more reasons to be bursting with unfathomable joy this day." Gabrielle stood and moved aside to let Liam approach. "You two beautiful young ladies are my daughters."

The girls stood and embraced their father, blinking through tears.

"Can you ever forgive me?" Gabrielle asked her daughters. They could, and they did. "We were in sin," Gabrielle admitted, "and that sin remained hidden all these years…until now."

"Be sure your sin will find you out," Liam sighed. "God's forgiveness and mercy for my wrongdoing is the reason I branded this ranch with the *Circle M* symbol." His eyes were moist as he looked at Marrin. "I overheard you praying in the barn one day." Marrin sucked in her breath sharply. "You are closer to God than most." His voice caught.

"No, that's not true," Marrin protested, wiggling self-consciously.

He held up a hand. "It is true. '…Be ye kind one to another, tenderhearted, forgiving one another, even as God for Christ's sake hath forgiven you.' That's Ephesians 4:32. I forgive both you girls as God has forgiven me." He peered up at Gabrielle. "I forgive you, too. You were a victim as much as I." He smiled at Marrin and Carina. "But we are victorious now, by the grace of God."

A span of emotional silence passed.

"So, Marrin is not my real sister or cousin or anything?" Robinette asked meekly, standing on trembling legs.

"Oh, no!" Marrin jumped up and held tightly to Robinette. "You will always be my sister. My little Robin bird. And we were raised and loved by your true mother and father, who were my parents as much as yours. Good parents."

Carina introduced her fiancé, Anton, to Marrin just as Edith entered the parlor to invite everyone into the dining room for breakfast, where they all spent the next few hours enjoying a warm meal, laughter, and many stories—catching up on missed years and discovering the threads that now tied their lives together.

After a whirlwind day of revelations, Marrin escaped the house, her heart full and her thoughts tangled. The sun dipped low in the freshly rinsed sky after a summer thunderstorm. Inhaling the clean, sweet breath of juniper berries, she stumbled through tall pasture grass that squeaked beneath her boots until she crested a small hill and fell to her knees out of sight of Mr. Stinson's tall, pink mansion. Not fully knowing why she needed to do so, she entwined her fingers in tufts of slippery grass and let out a primal scream that offered some release from the tumult of confusion in her anguished soul.

"Maman, Papa, I miss you!" she cried, letting the tears flow. "Robinette and I were your daughters. You loved us so purely, I never knew that Robinette and I weren't blood sisters. I never knew you weren't my blood parents. No one could ever love me the way you did. I should be happy that Mr. Stinson and Mademoiselle Dumont are my parents, but you were always my real mother and father. I love you so much." She dropped her face into her cold hands. "I still miss you."

Allowing herself the luxury of a good cry, Marrin finally rose shakily to her feet. Exhaustion was heavy on her as she continued walking aimlessly over the rolling fields.

So many questions wound around every thought—was this truly her home now? Could she see Mr. Stinson as a father? Though she understood Mademoiselle Dumont's circumstances, a pang of loss lingered. Yet amidst it all, she felt a quiet gratitude for the love that had found her at last.

Wandering back to the edge of the pond, Marrin spied a man casting the spider-silk flash of a fly rod line over the rippling, storm-gray water.

George. After his declaration of love to her the night before, Marrin had tried in vain to keep him out of her mind. Did he now know about her relationship to Liam and Gabrielle? If he did, would it change his view of Liam? Of her? Would he still care for her now that he knew she was born outside of marriage? Yet he, too, was born out of wedlock. What a complicated mess their lives were.

He smiled at her and wavered in a brief moment of indecision before reeling in his line and placing his rod on the ground before turning and walking along the grassy shoreline to her.

"Marrin," he said, his voice hoarse and whispered. "How are you after learning…all of this about…everything?"

Marrin hauled in a lungful of air. "I don't know. I really don't know."

He sucked his lower lip between his teeth, and his eyes reflected kindness and concern. "Have you thought at all about what I told you last night?"

"I don't know what to think of that either."

"I haven't changed my mind. I really do love you."

"Still?"

"Yes, still."

She shifted her weight uncomfortably and dropped her eyes to the ground. "I'm not sure I deserve to be loved by you. I've done so many wrong things, and now I'm finding out my birth parents weren't married when I was born and—"

"You remember I told you it was the same with my parents?" She nodded. "I'm not sure I deserve you, actually." She slowly raised her head, and her eyes met his.

"Why would you say that?" George asked. She looked at the ground and kicked a stone with the toe of her boot. "Marrin, I misjudged you and didn't treat you with the respect and honor you deserve." He paused to swallow. "I should have asked to hear your side of the story."

"Maybe we don't deserve each other," she said.

"But maybe we do." He chuckled gently. "What's really strange is that Liam is both your real father and my stepfather."

Marrin shivered. "Nor should we invite anyone to overthink it."

"Certainly not." He tucked a curl behind her ear. "Would you let me love you, Marrin? And would you consider loving me too?"

A smile tugged at the corner of her mouth. "I might consider it…if you call me by my nickname again."

He moved so quickly, she wasn't sure how she was suddenly engulfed in his warmth, the cinnamon-leather scent of his skin, the rough hardness of his bare arms. She nuzzled her nose into his chest until she felt his fingers touch her chin and lift her face to his.

His mouth pressed to her lips, slowly at first; then eagerly. He stopped kissing her and whispered into her ear: "Sparky." She almost laughed aloud.

But as he held her tightly, her body relaxed, melting into his embrace until she could no longer distinguish her own heart from his. In that moment, she felt safe, connected, accepted. And truly loved. Maybe they did deserve each other.

And she confessed that she really did love him.

Epilogue

"He felt that the world was not so hollow as he had believed." –Mark Twain, *Tom Sawyer*

1895

Not every story ends in perfect happiness—but some find a better ending than expected.

After returning to Greenwind Ranch, Carina and Marrin gradually adjusted to calling Gabrielle and Liam "Mother" and "Father." Reunited sisters Marrin and Robinette shared a bedroom in the big pink gingerbread house. Carina had a room of her own. Gabrielle settled into a small cottage near St. Mark's Episcopal Church in Yreka.

Carina's engagement to Anton, however, was not meant to be. After staying only a few more days at Greenwind, he broke things off and returned to Belgium, leaving Carina in fits of hysterics and melancholy. Marrin feared her sister might sail after Anton, but instead, she quickly found unexpected love again—this time with a young banker in town, named Edward. They were soon planning a hasty summer wedding, with Liam and Gabrielle urging them to wait another year to get to know each other first. They reluctantly complied.

Liam forgave Gabrielle for hiding his daughters from him. He'd learned again and again that unforgiveness only gnawed at the soul and threatened to turn his heart to stone. He also knew he was still in love with the lovely woman and, at Marrin and Carina's insistent prompting, he finally got up the courage to ask her to marry him, and the couple was married the following spring.

Marrin and George's wedding morning dawned bright, the sun piercing a slight mist of late-May rain. The ceremony took place beside the ranch pond with its rippling waves glistening like diamonds. Mt. Shasta gleamed with an anointing of fresh snow, and wild geese honked noisily overhead as the couple exchanged vows.

Thanks to the money Marrin had recovered from Alard, along with the reward money Liam insisted she keep, the newlyweds had a tidy little nest egg for starting their life together. They honeymooned in Crescent City, enjoying the splendor of the foggy coastal town, long walks on the beach, and the famed California redwoods.

On their return trip by train and stagecoach, George read *Tom Sawyer* and *Huckleberry Finn* aloud to his new bride, translating the text to French as needed. Marrin thoroughly enjoyed the stories, just as George had promised she would.

"I do not wish any reward but to know I have done the right thing," Marrin said, quoting Mark Twain. "Huckleberry was a naughty boy when he said that, but I like the words." She closed the book in George's lap, set it aside, and tugged his face to hers. "I know I've done the right thing," she said, smiling as she kissed him playfully.

It had taken a while for God to prove His existence to Marrin, but she could certainly see His hand and guidance in her life—even from birth.

After a blissful honeymoon along the Northern California coast, Marrin and George returned to Greenwind Ranch just in time to celebrate Carina's wedding in June.

And Gabrielle and Liam announced that they had officially adopted Robinette as their daughter, adding even more festivity to the day.

Marrin and George lived at Greenwind Ranch, enjoying the warmth of family and the peaceful rhythm of ranch life—and Marrin happily completed another term at the little schoolhouse in Yreka. In the spring of 1895, Liam approached them with a generous gift—a parcel of land for their own home, complete with the promise of his ranch hands to help build it.

"What do you think, Sparky?" asked George as they walked alongside the Shasta River one sunny afternoon, after dismounting from their horses to let them graze along the grassy banks.

Marrin shielded her eyes as she scanned the length of the river winding lazily through a small, lush valley. "C'est beau," she said. "It's beautiful."

"What would you think about building a house here for us?" George asked, his handsome grin breaking loose despite his best efforts.

Marrin's heart stopped. "What are you saying?"

"I'm saying that Liam is giving us this parcel for our own home, if we want it."

Marrin's eyes sparkled. "Is it true? He'd really do that?"

George laughed. "He would, and he's done exactly that already. He even said he'd lend us some of his ranch hands to help me build."

"Oh, George, it's too wonderful to be true. I mean, how God has turned my life around and…"

"And mine too," George added, snugging his arm about her waist.

"God has been too good to me," said Marrin.

"Not *too* good," said George. "Just good."

"I need to kiss you right now," Marrin whispered, giggling.

"I'll never say no to that," George laughed, "unless you've just eaten garlic."

Marrin ignored his teasing. Standing on her toes, she clasped her hands behind his neck and kissed him passionately, still surprised by the tingling that surged through her body and heart whenever she was close to him.

As a herd of horses thundered in the distance, Marrin lifted her eyes to heaven, mouthing thanks for God's liberation and His love that had caught her at last.

Author's Historical Note

A few historical details are woven throughout *Marrin's Masquerade. At the time of this writing, I live in rural Shasta Valley, between the two small towns of Montague and Yreka, California in rural Siskiyou County. I wrote more about Yreka than Montague in this book, because I live closer to this town. I imagined the setting for the Stinson house, where our home is located, but I moved the Shasta River closer and added a pond for ambience.*

Yreka is situated just off Interstate 5, south of the Oregon border. Many of Yreka's original historic buildings are still in existence. I mentioned the one-room schoolhouse, dubbed the "Red Church Skool House" in some writings. The charming little building is located on Ranch Lane south of Yreka near Greenhorn Park.

Mr. Liam Stinson's home was inspired by a large and charming historic Victorian home in Etna, California, which is painted a bright coral pink with forest green gingerbread trim.

The wild horses running free on the plains of the valley are true to life and fashioned after wild herds that still roam these parts, running free with majestic Mt. Shasta in the background.